PUFFIN BOOKS
CARAVAN TO TIBET

Deepa Agarwal has written about forty books in English
and Hindi, mostly for children. Among her recent titles are
*Anita and the Game of Shadows, Not Just Girls!, My Book of
Creative Writing* and *King Vikram and the Riddles of the
Vetal*. She is the author of a popular series of picture books
that includes titles like *Lippo Goes to the Park* and *Squiggly
Goes to School*. A regular contributor to children's magazines
both in India and abroad, she has edited and compiled a
number of anthologies as well.

Deepa has received many prestigious national awards for
her writing, including the NCERT National Award for
Children's Literature for her picture book *Ashok's New Friends*,
in 1992–93.

Deepa lives in Delhi with her husband and has three grown-
up daughters.

CARAVAN TO TIBET

Deepa Agarwal

Illustrations by Manobhiram Chakravarti

PUFFIN BOOKS

PUFFIN BOOKS

Published by the Penguin Group

Penguin Books India Pvt. Ltd, 11 Community Centre, Panchsheel Park, New Delhi 110 017, India

Penguin Group (USA) Inc., 375 Hudson Street, New York, New York 10014, USA

Penguin Group (Canada), 90 Eglinton Avenue East, Suite 700, Toronto, Ontario, M4P 2Y3, Canada (a division of Pearson Penguin Canada Inc.)

Penguin Books Ltd, 80 Strand, London WC2R 0RL, England

Penguin Ireland, 25 St Stephen's Green, Dublin 2, Ireland (a division of Penguin Books Ltd)

Penguin Group (Australia), 250 Camberwell Road, Camberwell, Victoria 3124, Australia (a division of Pearson Australia Group Pty Ltd)

Penguin Group (NZ), 67 Apollo Drive, Rosedale, Auckland 0632, New Zealand (a division of Pearson New Zealand Ltd)

Penguin Group (South Africa) (Pty) Ltd, 24 Sturdee Avenue, Rosebank, Johannesburg 2196, South Africa

Penguin Books Ltd, Registered Offices: 80 Strand, London WC2R 0RL, England

First published in Puffin by Penguin Books India 2007

Text copyright © Deepa Agarwal 2007
Illustrations copyright © Penguin Books India 2007

All rights reserved

10 9 8 7 6 5 4 3 2

ISBN 9780143330127

Typeset in Garamond Light by Eleven Arts, New Delhi
Printed at Yash Printographics, Noida

For my parents
who brought me up to love
both books and mountains

CONTENTS

ACKNOWLEDGEMENTS

It's hard to know where to begin—so many people have contributed in so many ways to this book. First, I'd like to gratefully acknowledge the late Rosalind Wilson's invaluable input, which played a crucial role in shaping the original 'Caravan to Tibet' when it first appeared as a long short story in the *Target Annual* while she was editor. A big thanks to Deborah Vetter, executive editor of the Cricket Magazine Group, who added her expertise when it was published in *Cricket* magazine in the same form. When I decided to develop it into a novel, her critical feedback was useful beyond words.

To go back further, I'd like to thank my cousin Wg Cdr R.S. Rawat for supplying the seed idea for this story with his fascinating accounts of his trips to Milam, plus photographs which helped me to visualize the setting, not to mention the various books he lent me from time to time. And even earlier, Pangtey Auntie and Joyce Auntie's enthralling narratives of family history served to spark my imagination. Cousin Harish Rawat, grandson of the famous explorer Pandit Kishan Singh and a well-known mountaineer himself, and his wife Kaushalya bhabhi provided extremely important information about Shauka customs, the trade expeditions and a host of other details. My sister Prema Rawat Popkin helped with books that provided useful data, as did the photographs from her treks. Thanks too to my cousin Jaya Gupta for her prompt response to a request for information.

Several books provided the essential historical facts without which this story could not have been written. Among them are *Indian Explorers of the Nineteenth Century* by Indra Singh Rawat; *Madhya Himalaya ki Bhotia Janjati: Johar ke Shauka* by Dr S.S. Pangtey; *Western Tibet and the Indian Borderland* by Charles A. Sherring; *The Pundits* by Derek Waller; *Lost World Tibet* by Amaury de Riencourt and *Kailash-Mansarovar* by Swami Pranavanand.

My husband Dilip supported me during the writing of this book in ways too many to recount, so did my daughters Garima, Sonali and Geetika—my sounding boards and hand-holders! I'd also like to thank my cousin Tripta Sabharwal and her husband Ravi Sabharwal for organizing the trip to Munsiari (more background) and providing lively company. Thanks too to Heather Delabre for boosting my morale when I badly needed it.

Finally I'd like to express my appreciation to Sudeshna for her meticulous editing of the manuscript and her excellent suggestions, and to Ajanta for her patience and cooperation.

And if in case I've left anyone out—please be kind enough to forgive the lapse.

AUTHOR'S NOTE

Caravan to Tibet is deeply rooted in my own family history and Debu's journey into Tibet is one that my ancestors actually undertook every year.

I grew up in Almora, a small town in Uttaranchal, but knew that my grandfather came from a place much further north, where life was quite different from our rather staid middle-class existence. Male cousins who undertook the trek to Milam to learn more about their origins returned with enthralling tales. (Girls were considered too delicate to make the trip!) They told us about the nomadic lifestyle, the annual trade expeditions, the explorers Pandit Nain Singh and Kishan Singh Rawat, and other members of our extended family who had mapped Tibet disguised as lamas in the nineteenth century. Some of my aunts, and occasionally my father, would add to that material. Though our connections with that past had become limited, the colourful rugs or chutkas that Debu tries to sell were part of our household furnishings along with the silver-lined wooden bowls Sonam Darka uses in the book. And uncles or cousins from the village would visit as well, occasionally making the journey on horseback.

All these accounts were so fascinating, that when I took up writing as a profession, I just had to put them into a story. 'Caravan to Tibet' first appeared in the children's magazine *Target* in 1989. Much later, I decided to expand it into an adventure novel, and am very happy that it has found a home with Puffin Books.

Certain political events led to the end of the trade expeditions in the 1950s, and the Shauka traders have adopted other professions. However, I do hope I have succeeded in providing a glimpse of those exciting times and that my readers enjoy this adventure story.

THE AMULET

There was something different in the air today, Debu thought, something that smelt of good things to come. Maybe he was imagining it, being over-hopeful as usual. How often had his father warned him—don't expect too much and you won't be disappointed. But Debu had never been able to follow that advice.

Perhaps it was the pilgrims crowding the village market who made him anticipate good business. They were passing through the village on their way back from a pilgrimage to the holy Mount Kailash and Lake Mansarovar, the abode of Lord Shiva. Most of the men were obviously from regions further south, with their large eyes and sharp features, so different from Debu's own people, the Shaukas.

Did they have enough money left over to spend? Please, Devi Ma, Debu whispered, praying to the goddess who was his family deity. Please. Make them buy a few rugs. You know how hard up we are right now.

'We haven't sold anything yet,' his younger brother Hayat said, squatting on the ground next to Debu. Hayat was ten to Debu's fourteen and his chubby face was turning crimson in the July heat. He began to pull off the white woollen coat he wore over his tight-fitting trousers. Though their village Milam, located on the India–Tibet border, stood at a height of over 11,000 feet, the thin air made the sun harsh. It was their summer home. The nomadic Shaukas travelled with their herds, spending winter in the low reaches of Quithi and spring in beautiful Munsiari.

'You should call out to them!' Hayat said.

Debu's high cheekbones flamed with anger. 'I know what to do!' he said coldly. 'And you'd better not forget who's in charge!' Hayat glowered but his full mouth trembled slightly.

Debu suppressed a sigh. He took off his round cap and let the breeze riffle through his thatch of wiry black hair. He was not sure if he enjoyed it—being the man of the house. If only his father would return. Worse, he knew Hayat was right. Just prayers wouldn't do. He had to coax customers to buy their wares. How he hated it! But he had to. These rugs, which his mother had woven, provided a good portion of their income.

A pair of enormous leather boots halted before him. A stout man stood there, pointing at a rug. 'How much for that chutka, boy?' he asked.

'Only ten rupees, sahib,' Debu's smile reduced his narrow eyes to slits. He unrolled the rug swiftly and forced himself to turn salesman. 'Feel the wool sahib, see the brilliant colours!'

'Ten! What do you think you're selling? Gold brocade? Not a paisa more then five!'

'Remember what Ma said! Get a good price!' Hayat had recovered his spirits enough to jab Debu in the ribs.

Ignoring him, Debu said, 'Sahib, give us seven at least.'

The man hesitated.

'It's a bargain,' Auntie Durga said. The elderly lady who sat next to them had silken-soft pashmina shawls stacked before her. 'See how skilfully it's woven, as well as any from Persia or Bukhara.'

'Perhaps you're right.' The man laughed. 'I'll take it, boy.'

'Here, sahib!' Debu rolled up the rug and counted the silver coins the man handed him. A rush of elation warmed him. He had barely put the cash away when a shadow blocked the sunlight. He glanced up hopefully, then stiffened. It wasn't a customer, but his father's cousin Trilok.

Short, bow-legged, with a straggly moustache and unkempt hair, Cousin Trilok had a permanent frown. Even at that early hour, a strong odour of chhang, the local beer, wafted from him.

'Hunhh . . . so . . . you gettin' lotta money,' he growled. 'When're you plannin' to return mine?'

'We don't owe you anything,' Debu tried to ignore

3

the thumping in his chest. 'That matter's been settled by the elders.' He gulped. 'Uncle Kalyan swore that my father repaid the money he borrowed from you.'

'What does th't fool know? How can those dodderin' elders settle my concerns?' Trilok snarled. 'Tell your mother to return the money fast—or—or she'll be sorry.'

'Keep your mouth shut, you drunken idiot!' Auntie Durga's sharp voice sliced through the noise.

'Who're you to tell me!' His bleary eyes glinted. 'J'st wait till September, boy, and I'll teach you how to behave!'

He lurched away. A red hot rage roared in Debu's ears. 'Don't bother,' Auntie Durga said quickly. 'Half the time the fool's not in his senses.'

Debu tried to nod and let his breathing even out. But the question continued to throb in his head. How could they get rid of Cousin Trilok? Should they pay him off? His mother refused to. Her reply was always the same: 'Your father cleared that debt. He's just trying to take advantage of his absence.'

Debu sighed again. The scene of the caravan's return from Tibet last year rose up like an unwanted ghost. The excited cries of the other children, 'They're back! They're back!'; the women hurrying towards the path that sloped down to the village, giggling, crooning songs of welcome. And then . . . the grim faces of the men riding back from the trading trip—Uncle Kalyan Singh, Bijay Singh, Jeevan and . . . Cousin Trilok's sly smirk.

He had continued to gaze at the empty path after all the ponies, the load-bearing jibbos and yaks had straggled in, waiting for his father to appear. Something

4

must have delayed him. A load that slipped off, a stone in a horse's shoe, anything could hold a man up for a few minutes. He kept waiting even when the voices hushed suddenly and the men went into a huddle with the headman, the Boorah.

The pitying looks didn't register at all. It couldn't be anything to do with them, he thought. Then the Boorah summoned him. 'There's bad news, son. You must bear it like a man. You have to take care of your mother and your younger brother now . . .'

The words didn't make sense even when Kalyan Singh, never a man to show much emotion, spoke, repeatedly running a tongue over his cracked lips. 'It was a terrible storm, son. Just don't know what happened. How Dharma got lost. The snow made it impossible to see. You're a brave boy, I know.' He'd squeezed his shoulder and jerked away.

It was Jeevan, the youngest of the group, who'd held Debu close when he'd yelled, 'No! It's not true! He's going to come back. I know it. I know it!'

'Hush,' he'd said. 'Hush . . .' Jeevan's smell had reminded him of Baujyu's when he returned from Tibet. That mixture of old sweat, leather, horseflesh, overlaid with the tang of the junipers and the scent of herbs growing in the high meadows they passed through before entering the village. And Debu had found it hard to hold back the shameful tears that had flowed and flowed from his eyes.

He remembered the date well—17 September 1891—from the English calendar his father had brought from Calcutta. He had gone there the previous winter to buy goods to trade in Tibet. 'We need to learn the new ways that the white men have introduced,' he had said. 'We need to keep up with the times.'

'Tell me about your journey,' Debu had said. That sounded far more thrilling than the calendar. 'Tell me about the train, the huge iron horse. Can it really carry hundreds of people?'

'Yes,' Baujyu had smiled. 'The fire in its belly helps it to run faster than any real horse can.'

'Weren't you scared, Baujyu?'

'No!' His father had said dismissively. Debu knew he rarely was. And now, Debu was sure he was not frightened when the caravan ran into the storm. Which meant that somehow his father must have escaped. But Debu was often afraid. He was afraid that Ma and Hayat might have to go hungry. Afraid that they'd always be poor, and most of all he was afraid that he might end up with Cousin Trilok as his stepfather.

According to a custom in their tribe his mother might be asked to remarry their closest male relative—Cousin Trilok—if his father didn't return. And time was beginning to run out. In barely three months it would be a year since the caravan returned. If his father wasn't found by then, the Boorah would declare him officially dead.

No, Debu thought, Baujyu was definitely alive. Something told him he was. But how could he prove it? If only he could fly to Tibet like the Shaukia Lama who had winged his way to this valley in ancient times and settled his people here.

'That man's looking this way,' Hayat nudged him. 'Rugs, beautiful rugs for sale! Come and buy, at unbelievable prices!' he called out.

The man was so amused at Hayat's antics that he bought their largest rug. And as the day progressed and sales were brisk, Debu's heart lifted.

'All right,' he told Hayat finally. They had sold most of their rugs by now. 'You're the best salesman here. Come, let's get the wool and spices for Ma.'

Debu glanced up at the sky as he rose. The sunlight was paling and clouds beginning to huddle behind the mountains. They would have to hurry with their shopping.

It was a struggle to keep his mind focussed as they walked through the noise of the market. He glanced distractedly at the trinkets some traders from the south were selling, at the farm implements and bales of printed cotton cloth. Pyramids of dried red chillies spread their sting in the air. Then a familiar soothing aroma calmed him down. It reminded him of lentils cooking, of the healing paste his mother had applied to his foot when he hurt it last year. Quickly, he stooped to pick up a handful of yellow turmeric roots. Ma had said that their stock of this very essential spice was running low.

'Debu!' Hayat pulled at his coat sleeve. 'I want some candy!' He pointed to a trader who had white lumps of mishri, the local candy, along with golden-brown discs of jaggery, the coarse sugar they used as sweetening.

'Later,' Debu said impatiently. 'We have to buy wool first . . . *Phew*!' He wrinkled his short, blunt nose as the overpowering odour of asafoetida wafted towards him. 'There they are!' It was the Tibetans who usually sold this flavouring, as well as the raw wool the boys needed. They turned towards the broad-faced men with wispy plaits hanging down their backs.

'Friend,' Debu approached a large man with a wide-brimmed hat perched on his head. 'What price for your wool?'

'Two annas for one seer in weight,' the man grinned. The sun and wind had marked his face with tiny lines and polished his high cheekbones into a ruddy flush. He held up a fluffy wad of wool.

Debu rubbed it between his fingers, trying to look knowledgeable. 'Too much, Uncle! The rate is only one anna.'

The man laughed, making his chunky turquoise and coral earring shiver. Debu watched amused, then gasped. He stared at the amulet around the man's neck. A golden 'om', a lucky rudraksh bead and two carved corals on each side, strung on a black cord. It was just like . . .

'You're sharp, boy. Sharp for your age.' The singsong voice brought him back. 'How much do you want?'

'At least forty seers,' Debu's eyes remained fixed on the Tibetan's throat.

'What are you gaping at?' the man frowned.

'The amulet! Where did you get it?'

'What is it to you?' the Tibetan's voice was gruff.

'My father was lost in a blizzard last year, crossing the Kungri Bingri Pass,' Debu said breathlessly. 'He—he used to wear an amulet just like that.'

'Oh-h,' the man's eyes widened. 'I bought it in Gartok.'

'Gartok?' Hayat exclaimed. Gartok was the chief town of western Tibet, one of the places where the Shaukas traded.

'Can—can I look at it?' Debu asked, his heart pounding like the blacksmith's hammer. So similar . . . Suppose it actually *was* Baujyu's?

'All right.' The man unwound the amulet from his neck and handed it to Debu. Eagerly the boys studied the corals. Their father had got them from Nepal. Holy words were carved on them . . . and . . . one of them was slightly damaged. The amulet had dropped off while his father was loading a mule and the animal stepped on it. Debu turned the beads around shakily, and caught his breath—one coral was chipped at exactly the same place!

'It—it is Baujyu's!' he exclaimed.

'Yes! It is! It is!' Hayat shrieked. 'See this broken coral?'

The Tibetan flashed a puzzled smile. 'But Gartok is far from the pass. I wonder how the amulet got there . . .'

Gartok *was* far from the pass. If Baujyu had perished in the storm—surely it would have got buried

10

in the snow along with him! Goosebumps sprang up on Debu's skin.

'He *is* alive! I knew it!' He thrust the amulet back into the man's hand. 'I must tell my mother!' He was about to run off, when he recalled with a start that he had to pay for the wool.

'Quick! Go get Bijli!' he told Hayat, hastily counting out the coins.

Hayat hurried back with their pony, who was tethered close by. They began to load her.

The Tibetan's eyes widened. 'That's a Rudok pony!' he said, pointing at the pretty grey pony with the shaggy mane. Then he added reproachfully, 'She's meant for racing and you're using her for a pack animal.'

Debu's face darkened. He could guess why the Tibetan was upset. Bijli, who could run almost as fast as the lightning she'd been named after, *was* special. She came from a place in Tibet famous for its horses. 'We can't help it,' he said gruffly. 'Most of our jibbos were lost in the storm along with my father.'

The man's face softened and he nodded as he turned away.

They had almost reached the last stall when Hayat cried, 'What about my candy?'

'Oh-h! All right. Sorry, I forgot,' Debu said. Then his eye fell on a brightly coloured wooden top. 'And what about this?' he said. It had been a long time since they could even dream of indulging themselves. Hayat grinned as he grabbed the top.

But as they tramped home, Debu began to have

doubts. Should he tell Ma about the amulet? Sometimes he felt that she too believed that Baujyu might come back. She had even woven a length of woollen cloth for a coat and trousers for him, the way all wives did each year. However, she never shared her thoughts with Debu.

Would he be raising false hopes? But . . . how could he not tell? Because . . . the amulet was proof— proof that Baujyu lived. If they couldn't produce proof . . . Cousin Trilok would take control of their lives.

And that would be worse than losing Baujyu.

BREAKING THE NEWS

The familiar landmarks passed them one by one as they tramped home, but Debu's confusion persisted. Wistfully he glanced at the twin peaks of Hardeval and Trishuli, brilliantly white against the dimming azure of the sky. The terraced potato fields spread out like patches of green carpet, tender shoots of buckwheat and barley were sprouting. The rains had begun bountifully this year and the crops, planted on their arrival in Milam, barely a month ago, were doing well. The last beams of the disappearing sun turned the Goriganga river into a silver stream. But this well-loved sight brought little comfort.

Debu paused for a moment as they trudged up the rocky path that led to their home. A lilting strain of song reached his ear. It was Ma's voice, softening the rattle of the loom as she worked it. She sounded quite cheerful.

Impulsively, Debu turned to Hayat, 'You're not to say anything about the amulet. *I'll* tell her.'

Hayat opened his mouth to say something, but Debu's frown silenced him.

Ma was sitting in the paved courtyard, which was already dark with shadows. But a few beams of sunlight still warmed the grey stone walls of their long, narrow house, and picked out the finely carved doors and windows.

'There you are!' she cried. The skirt of her black ghaghra flared out from her slender waist as she rose. With a familiar gesture, she pulled up the white veil framing her pale, delicate face. A single necklace of silver coins glinted at her throat. Earlier she had worn so many that they hung to her knees. They had all gone, even the silver perfume case that had swung at her waist, which Debu loved to sniff when he was younger. Gone to pay for food, fuel and the other things they needed to survive.

'Ma, Ma!' Hayat cried out. 'We sold most of the rugs and I got some candy and a top!'

Ma's face crinkled in a smile. 'Is that true?' she asked. 'Devi Ma be praised. But come, have something to eat first.'

She hurried into the kitchen, a low-roofed cabin on one side of the house, while Debu led Bijli into the stable. The sight of the empty stalls on the ground floor of the house still made him gloomy. He was so used to the sounds of the jibbos—mules gentle as the

14

cows and hardy as the yaks they were bred from—which were kept there.

A kettle was already simmering on the wood fire. Ma quickly poured tea, spiced with ginger, into gleaming brass tumblers. 'You must be really hungry.' Her face grew pinched. 'I wish I had something better than this wretched sattu.'

Debu frowned at Hayat who was making a face. 'Oh, Ma! You know we love it,' he said. There was actually something comforting about the roasted barley flour, which he stirred into a paste with the hot tea before devouring it. It was what they always ate, on their constant journeys, from the pleasant valley of Quithi in winter, Munsiari in spring, Milam in summer and then back again in reverse order.

'Agh-gh!' A huge yawn split Hayat's face as he rose from his low wooden stool.

'You've had a long day,' Ma said, picking up the oil lantern she had just lit. 'Get to bed now.'

Debu's legs felt heavy as he followed her up the steep stairs to the second floor, stooping to enter the low doorway. Hayat was already snuggling in his cotton quilt. Ma laid a striped woollen blanket over it for extra warmth, even though the single small window was tightly shut. A couple of deerskin trunks, in which they stored their valuables, completed their bedroom furniture along with the worn out rugs, which covered the beaten mud floor.

Exhausted, Debu was about to lie down too when he sat up with a jerk. 'I haven't given you the money,' he said.

15

'Thirty-three rupees!' she exclaimed, counting out their earnings. 'This'll keep us for quite some time.'

'Auntie Durga saved a good place for us,' Debu said. 'And a large group of pilgrims was passing through.'

'She's a dear soul,' Ma said. 'But . . . why've you been so quiet since you came?'

Debu took a deep breath. 'Ma,' he said, his eyes fixed on the ground, 'I—I saw Baujyu's amulet with a Tibetan!'

Hayat sprang up in bed, wide awake now.

Ma went as white as her veil. 'What—what are you saying? Are you sure?'

'Both of us saw it,' Debu said. 'It *is* his.'

'Yes!' Hayat broke in. 'It had a chipped coral bead like Baujyu's. The man said he'd bought it in Gartok.'

'Gartok? How did it get there?' Ma's voice was faint.

'I don't know . . .' Debu shook his head. 'But don't you see? It means that Baujyu might have survived the blizzard.'

His mother clutched her veil closer to her face. 'I don't know if it does . . .' She almost choked on the words.

'Ma . . . I—I think it's a sign—that he's alive and well.' Debu's exasperation buzzed in his throat.

'If he is alive, why didn't he return?'

'Who knows why? Why he couldn't make it back with one of the caravans that returned later . . .'

'Maybe he'll come back this time,' Hayat said.

But Ma just shook her head. 'I wonder . . .' she said with a sigh. 'Come, let's go to bed,' she went on. 'We have to get up early to hoe the fields.' She squeezed

16

Debu's arm gently. 'It's been hard. But let's not mislead ourselves with false hopes.'

'No!' Debu said, almost jerking his arm away. 'We cannot ignore this sign. Don't you want him back?'

Ma stared at him in disbelief. Debu bit his lip and looked away. If only he could control his temper. It was a relief when Ma spoke again.

'Even if it is your father's,' she said, 'it may not be proof enough for the elders, son.'

Miserably, Debu nodded, acknowledging the truth of her words. But how could they—the family—ignore such an important sign? A sudden thought shot through his head.

'Ma . . . the Sarje came just a few days ago!' he cried.

'Yes,' Hayat said. 'I saw him—the messenger from Tibet! He had lots of sheep with him. And the headman greeted him with drums and pipes playing.'

'He said that the passes are open and we are free to take our caravan to Tibet,' Debu continued. 'He even checked to see if the animals are free from disease.'

'The headman shook his hand, and asked him if all was well in his country,' Hayat said importantly. 'Then the headman picked up a large stone and broke it. He gave half of it to the Sarje to take back. And lots of candy and many other things.'

'I heard,' Ma said. Her eyes were wary, as if she'd already guessed what Debu was about to say.

'Ma!' he said. 'You know what this means. The caravan will be leaving soon. I want to go too and look for Baujyu!'

17

'*You*! But you're too young! Do you know how hard the journey is? The dangers! No, no!' She shook her head emphatically. 'If he has survived, he'll return on his own.'

'But I have to find out, make sure! Suppose he's unable to come back for some reason! What then?'

Hayat's shrill interruption almost covered up the tremor that shook Ma's slight frame. 'Yes!' he cried. 'Ma, we have to find out if Baujyu's there. Otherwise you'll have to marry that horrible Cousin Trilok!'

'Quiet!' Debu hissed.

'But—but that's what everyone says!' Hayat said sulkily.

Ma's face turned stony. Desperate to end the silence, Debu said, more brusquely than he intended, 'I'm used to hard journeys—you know that, Ma. I can even speak Tibetan quite well by now . . . and . . . I'm not a child, Ma . . . I'm taller than Uncle Kalyan Singh!' Then somewhat defiantly, 'The Boorah said I was supposed to take care of you all. Decide what's to be done!'

When Ma still did not reply, Debu said, 'Please, Ma! I can carry some goods to sell too. We can make some decent money.' He continued in a softer voice, 'Please! Can't you understand? You have to!'

Ma held his gaze for a while. Then she nodded. 'All right,' she said. 'If you feel you must. But I don't know if they'll take you.'

'Let me ask at least!'

GIVE ME A CHANCE!

Had any night been longer, more restless? How Debu had longed for the day when he'd be old enough to join the trade caravan. He couldn't wait to find out if those fascinating things actually existed—the towering monasteries, the lamas with magical powers, and the huge markets where people from all over Central Asia came to trade. Was the journey as rigorous as they claimed? His people took pride in following the most dangerous route. They travelled through three treacherous passes, which had to be crossed in one day, no matter how harsh the weather. Merchants from other parts favoured less tricky ones, he'd heard.

But when he recalled Ma's words, anxiety surfaced. Would they let him join the expedition?

They will have to agree, he tried to reassure himself.

I have the strongest reason of all to go! I'll convince Uncle Kalyan Singh. He's the leader. He may be dour and forbidding, but Baujyu always insisted he was good at heart. When I tell him about the amulet, he'll definitely agree.

The moment he woke up, Debu rushed to meet Kalyan Singh. The bony, wrinkled man was busy supervising arrangements for the trip. Sacks of wheat flour, lentils and barley flour, cakes of jaggery sugar and candy, bales of cloth and other items lay around—provisions for the journey and goods to trade with the Tibetans.

His mother's cousin Bijay Singh was there too along with one or two other men. He sat on a low stool, making lists with a bamboo pen. Debu cast an admiring glance at his smart coat, a sharp contrast to Kalyan Singh's frayed old one. Bijay was known for his dandified ways. Well, Uncle Kalyan was not a man to spend an extra paisa, even though he was one of the richest men in the village.

Debu put his palms together and bowed to all of them. 'Uncle,' he said, turning to Kalyan Singh. Suddenly, a swarm of doubts plugged his mouth.

'What is it, Debu? Is your mother well? Do—do you need anything?' Kalyan Singh's gravelly voice was unusually gentle.

Why am I scared, Debu wondered. Hasn't he, hasn't everyone always been kind to us since Baujyu got lost?

He gulped, took a deep breath, then the words gushed out. 'Uncle, I want to join the caravan. I want to go to Tibet. To search for my father!'

Kalyan Singh's narrow eyes widened in surprise. Someone cried, 'What? Ho, what's the boy saying?'

Then the leader shook his head decisively. 'Son,' he said, 'I don't like to say this . . . but it's not possible that your father Dharma Singh escaped that terrible blizzard . . . There's no chance that you'll find him in Tibet. None at all.'

'But, Uncle,' Debu said, trying to hold fast, despite those discouraging words. 'I've found proof—proof that he survived. I—I saw his amulet with a Tibetan yesterday!'

'What? No, no!' Kalyan Singh shook his head again. 'No one could have lived through that storm. We were lucky to make it, and he was alone. And . . . even if the amulet is his—it's no proof that he's alive. In any case,' he continued, 'you're too young.'

Debu's full mouth set stubbornly. 'It *is* his amulet, Uncle. I know it is. I'm sure he's alive. As for being too young . . . you know I'm as strong as any grown-up man.' It sounded disrespectful, he knew, but he was beyond caring.

'Strong he is,' said stocky Jeevan, who was helping to pack the provisions. Barely twenty, he had joined the expedition just last year. '*Uh-ho*, Debu!'

A moment later, Debu was struggling to hold on to a sack full of flour Jeevan had hurled at him! He just about managed to catch it. It must have weighed at least forty seers, and almost knocked him over. Breathing hard, he put it down, smiling.

'What do you think you're doing?' Kalyan Singh yelled. 'Playing with our goods!'

'He's mad, crazy,' Bijay Singh shook his head, frowning. 'Still so irresponsible.' He took a pinch of snuff from a brocade pouch and sniffed delicately.

'*Uh-ho*, Uncle. I knew he wouldn't drop it. Forgive me.' A deep dimple appeared in Jeevan's cheek as he bowed slightly. 'Didn't you see him handle that runaway horse last month?'

'He may be strong but he's still a child.' Bijay Singh pursed his thin lips. He added in a milder tone. 'Son, your father got lost . . . How will your mother bear it if something happens to you? And—and . . . if he survived, he will definitely try to join us when we get there.'

'You're right,' Kalyan Singh said, shaking his head. 'We've never taken such a young boy along. Son, I promise to search for your father thoroughly wherever we go.'

'But I can't wait that long! Don't be so hard, Uncle.' Debu hated himself for pleading like that, but he had to. 'There's always a first time for everything. I swear on my mother, I can take care of myself! Please let me go too!'

'Go where?' A vaguely familiar voice sounded in his ear.

Debu whirled around. It was the Tibetan. 'Go with the caravan,' he said eagerly, 'to find my father. See!' He pointed to the amulet. 'That's Baujyu's!'

Kalyan Singh peered at it. 'It does look like the one Dharma used to wear . . . Where did you get it from, Sonam Darka?'

'I bought it from a man at Gartok.' Sonam began to take it off. 'Keep it, son.'

'No, no,' Debu protested. 'You keep it, friend. You paid for it. It's enough that I've seen it. *Now* will you let me come, Uncle?'

'Take him, Kalyan Singh,' Sonam's voice was soft with sympathy. 'Give him a chance to find his father.' Debu gazed at the man, marvelling that he could be so understanding.

'But your mother?' Kalyan Singh asked.

'She's agreed,' Debu said. 'Hayat's there, so she won't be alone. And there's Auntie Durga—and everyone else.'

Kalyan Singh was silent for a while. 'You are a stubborn boy,' he said finally. 'All right. You can come. But mind, you'll have to keep up with the rest.'

'I will, I will. Thank you, Uncle,' Debu rushed to touch his feet. 'And . . . I'll do whatever work you want me to. Anything—just try me!'

Kalyan Singh placed a hand on his head, saying dryly, 'There'll be plenty to do. But remember, we leave in two days. You have very little time to prepare for the journey. You must be ready in time. And . . . I have to seek permission from the Boorah.'

'As you wish, Uncle. And I'll be ready tomorrow if you say so!' Debu said impatiently. He knew the headman wouldn't refuse if Kalyan Singh had agreed. He couldn't wait to give his mother the wonderful news. Mundane things like preparing for the journey were far from his mind!

GETTING SET

A dingy-grey sheet of cloud stretched across the sky when Debu came down from the temple the next morning. He glanced at it anxiously. Rain would add to the perils of their expedition.

His mother had told him to go there and pray to the Devi for a safe journey and success in his mission.

As he entered the courtyard he saw Hayat crouched on the ground spinning his new top. 'Why didn't you go to school?' Debu asked. In reply Hayat threw him an injured look.

'He said he wanted to spend time with you because you were going,' his mother replied. 'Come, wash your hands, you must be hungry.'

'Eh, won't you give me a chance?' Debu tried to mollify Hayat. Unsmiling, Hayat picked up the top and dropped it in Debu's hand. But when Debu began to spin the top on his palm, flung it in the air, then caught it again, Hayat laughed and clapped.

'Come, eat!' Ma urged. The boys washed their hands, then sat cross-legged on low wooden stools.

'Lamb curry and rice!' Debu exclaimed. His favourite meal—he hadn't enjoyed it for a long time.

'Eat well,' Ma said. 'You'll only get roasted barley flour and dried meat there and butter tea.'

'Don't the Tibetans eat rice and meat curry?' Hayat asked.

'It doesn't taste the same. Your father always complained that the meat, even the rice, remained half cooked. It was the height, he said,' Ma replied, putting big bowls of kheer before them.

'Take mine too,' Hayat picked out some fat raisins from his bowl.

'Are you sure?' Debu's throat felt tight. They always squabbled over the raisins! He was so stuffed now that he could hardly move. But there was a lot to be done.

'Will Bijli be able to manage the trip?' he asked his mother.

'Of course,' Ma smiled. 'She was much younger when she came, remember? And you'll be better off with a horse you know.'

Debu remembered the day his father had brought Bijli from Tibet. It felt as if it was just yesterday.

'You're spoiling the boy,' his mother had said.

But Baujyu had replied, 'Can't you see he has a way with horses? No boy in our clan can ride like that!' His strong-jawed face had glowed with pride . . .

I must take an extra thick blanket for her, Debu thought, sighing, and a good supply of grain. Jeevan said there wouldn't be too much fresh grass in Tibet.

'You can carry some of the rugs that remain,' she went on. 'If your father had been here . . . he would have gone down to the plains as usual in winter and bought cloth and spices to take.'

'We can get some jaggery too,' Debu said. He tried to sound enthusiastic. He had hardly any goods to trade with and if he didn't find his father . . . they'd be poorer than before. If there'd been time, he'd have borrowed money from the headman and gone to the nearest town to buy some provisions. Then a thought chilled him. 'Will Baujyu's partner acknowledge me?'

'Dawa Nangal is a good man,' his mother said. Too quickly, Debu thought. 'He knows you.'

'But suppose . . .

'Debu!' Ma's voice was sharp. 'Dawa has gone through the partnership ceremony with your father. As his son, you have the same rights!'

Debu was barely seven then. But he remembered how his father had poured beer, a symbol of water, into a silver bowl and touched it with gold, wool, butter and flour and both he and Dawa Nangal had sipped it. They had exchanged gifts and finally broken a stone into two. His father had kept one half and Dawa Nangal the other. In case of a dispute the two pieces would be put together to show that the partnership did exist. This was the ceremony known as 'shair chyun–dunl chyun'. Shair meant gold in Tibetan, dunl, silver and chyun, water. Water with gold and silver was considered a symbol of purity and transparency. All the traders had Tibetan partners who took care of their interests there.

'Is that piece of stone here?' he asked. 'The partnership stone?'

Ma rubbed her forehead. 'Perhaps your father took it on the journey,' she said slowly.

'Do you think he needed to?' Debu frowned.

'I—I don't know . . .' Ma looked troubled. 'And I'm not sure where he kept it either.' Then she brightened. 'We can search for it.'

They went through the two deerskin trunks that held all their belongings. They pulled each and everything out and looked again and again. But the stone was not there.

'He must have taken it,' Ma sighed. 'Don't worry. Everyone knows Uncle Dawa's your father's partner.'

Would that make a difference? Would Dawa Nangal accept a young boy as a partner? Debu could not shake off his doubts.

Suppose he refused to recognize him? If only he could find the stone!

He remained seated on the bed, lost in thought, while his mother returned to her loom and Hayat went out to play. As he gazed at the ground, a vague memory stirred. One night, perhaps a year ago, he had woken to see his father tiptoeing out of the room, lantern in hand. Debu felt curious, but didn't dare ask in case Baujyu got angry. There were things children were not supposed to know about. But he'd been unable to control himself and sneaked out after him. He'd followed his father to the stable and tried to peep in. However, his father shut the door. Debu waited outside for a while. He could hear the sound of digging quite clearly, beneath the animals' restless snorts. Then his fear and the cold had overpowered him and he'd crept back to bed.

Had his father been hiding the stone? Debu ran to the stable and picked up the spade that stood against the wall in a corner. Where should he begin? He closed his eyes and tried to recall what he had heard. The thud of earth being broken had seemed to come from the right side of the stable. Well, he had to begin somewhere! He picked up handfuls of the straw placed there to keep the animals warm, threw it aside and began to dig.

He dug and dug but couldn't find anything at all. Soon his arms became so sore that he was ready to give up. There was already a sizable pit before him . . . he couldn't tear up the whole stable . . . Frustrated, he jabbed the spade into the ground angrily, one last time.

A current shot up his arm. The shovel had struck something hard. Debu brushed the mud off eagerly to find—just a large piece of rock!

Irritated, he flung down the spade and dusted his hands. Then he forced himself to stop and think again. His father had definitely hidden something. Could the rock have been placed there to mislead thieves?

He pried the rock loose with the shovel and lifted it up. Then he removed more of the soil beneath. And then—the spade hit something solid again. Yes!

There was something there, with a definite shape—like—the rim of an earthen pot! He tore at the earth around the pot, loosened it, then pulled it out carefully. His hands shook so hard as he removed the cloth tied around its mouth that he was afraid he'd drop and break it. There was something inside—a leather bag. He lifted it out with an effort. It was heavy!

Debu's heart pounded like a crazy drum. With trembling fingers he untied the string around the opening to see what was inside. He shouted out so loud that his mother and Hayat came running.

'Look! Look what I've found!'

'The stone?' Hayat piped up.

'No! Not the stone, but something as important.'

'What could be as important?' Ma asked.

The first coin he pulled out slipped through his fingers and rolled away. Hayat jumped and grabbed it before it came to a standstill.

'A tanka,' his mother said, examining the coin. 'I was aware that your father had bought a stock of these to trade. I wonder why he left them behind.'

'I wonder too . . .' Debu's brow wrinkled. 'He had hidden them well.'

Tankas were silver coins used to pay taxes in Tibet. Traders often bought these coins at Calcutta and Kalimpong where they were sold at the rate of ten tankas to a rupee. At Gyanima, where the Johari Shaukas traded, they could be sold for three or four to a rupee—a profitable deal.

'But how did you think of searching here?' his mother asked, puzzled.

Quickly Debu narrated the incident. 'Now I have something to do business with!'

'But,' Hayat piped up, 'you didn't find the stone. Do you think it could be hidden there too?'

'The stone!' Debu had completely forgotten about it!

He groped inside the pot again. There *was* something else there. But . . . it didn't feel like a stone . . . It was another bag! A smaller one, made of yellow silk. It contained coins too! Debu unwound the string that held it shut while his mother and Hayat watched, their faces anxious. Wordlessly he held out another coin.

'Hai Rama! It's gold!' his mother cried.

Debu stared at this unexpected bonanza, too overcome to speak. To think it had been lying there all this time!

They finally decided that he should carry two hundred of the silver coins and keep the rest back— there were about seven hundred of them. There were twenty gold coins, which his mother said were guineas, British coins.

'You can use a gold coin to buy goods for the journey!' Hayat said excitedly.

'Yes,' Debu smiled. 'Now I won't have to borrow money from the headman.'

Debu kept another gold coin as an emergency fund for the journey. He would hide it in the sole of his boot, he decided. Carefully, they placed the remaining gold and silver coins back in their hiding place.

The rest of the day passed in hectic preparation.

Debu managed to purchase a stock of jaggery sugar and candy from a trader who had come up for the village market and couldn't sell all of it. Some printed cotton cloth too. When he finally lay down on his bed after dinner, he was exhausted. He slept so soundly that his mother had to shake him hard to wake him in the morning.

He gulped down a glass of tea and rushed off to seek Kalyan Singh's advice.

'Uncle,' he said. 'I only have one jibbo and not too many goods to trade.'

'Never mind. You are going to search for your father.'

'Eh, Debu, Dharma bought a large number of tankas the year before when we went to Calcutta together,' Jeevan said. 'I wonder if he took them all along.'

So the others knew about the hoard. Well, he'd need their help to sell the coins. All the same, Debu said, 'I—I'll ask my mother.'

'Do that,' Kalyan Singh said. 'They would come in very useful.'

'I h've a prior claim on those t'nkas!' It was Cousin Trilok's hateful voice. 'He b'rrowed money from me to buy them.'

'Which he paid back after he sold some of the coins last year at Gyanima,' Kalyan Singh said sternly.

'He didn't return it all,' Trilok Singh growled.

'As far as I can remember, he did,' Kalyan Singh said firmly. 'And I don't want to hear any more!'

Trilok turned away muttering something that the others chose to ignore. But Debu had to fight hard to control the churning in his stomach. When would this matter be settled? He had to find Baujyu to be free of this pest.

THE JOURNEY BEGINS

The caravan left early the next day—a cavalcade of yaks, jibbos, sheep and ponies. The yaks and jibbos were heavily laden with goods. So were the pack sheep, which had come with the Tibetans.

Much feasting preceded the departure. A lavish meal of lamb curry, potatoes, halwa—the sweet semolina pudding they all loved—and golden puris was laid out. They stuffed themselves, knowing it would be long before they ate so well.

Debu couldn't believe that he was off at last. He felt strangely numb despite the excitement around him. The loud voices of the men, the champing of the horses, the jingling of the bells on the animals' necks, all seemed far away. So did the music of drums and horns, heard above the droning of the priest chanting mantras to ensure their safety during the trip. The tiny bells the dancing girls wore on their feet jingled as he watched them dip and sway. But it seemed to be something in which he had no part. When Sonam Darka raised a cheery hand in greeting he could only manage a stiff smile.

Almost the whole village was there. When he bent to bow to the gathered elders, a chorus of good wishes echoed around him.

'Go with my blessings, son,' his mother embraced him, putting an auspicious red mark on his forehead. She waved a handful of rice and beans around his head to ward off bad luck, then flung them in a bush. As she drew away blinking back tears, Debu's throat choked up.

Hayat's eyebrows stretched up almost to his hairline when Debu bent to hug him. His hand crept into Debu's coat pocket. It was a parting gift—his new top! Debu's eyes grew misty. Quickly he moved away and heaved himself up to mount Bijli: a quivering Bijli whose legs danced restlessly. The enthusiasm had infected her too!

'May the gods make your path smooth, son!' he heard Auntie Durga call out.

He bowed to her and waved a last goodbye. Suddenly his stomach fluttered as if an impatient bird were trapped inside it, struggling to get free.

The others were hoisting themselves up on their horses too. Many carried guns and daggers. The way was infested with robbers and often bandit hordes would attack without warning and carry off the traders' goods. With a loud invocation to the god Ganesha, the remover of obstacles, the expedition set off.

The road wound up steeply through the short junipers and rhododendrons and an occasional birch rose like a white ghost between them. The valley stretched out behind him and the tall silent mountains loomed ahead. Uneven patches of snow still straggled in dark corners while mist floated between the hills and wound itself round the sparse evergreens.

Gravely Kalyan Singh called out 'Hari Om!' in his bass voice. Jeevan echoed the holy words and the others kept up the chorus, intoning 'Hari Om!' in a regular beat.

Debu chimed in too. His nervousness was replaced by an unexpected calm as his body kept pace with the chant and the rhythmic movement of Bijli's legs.

All of a sudden Mount Trishuli emerged before them, along with its twin peak, the sacred Mount Hardeval, silvery-bright against the blue sky. The men folded their hands and prayed to Hardeval to protect their animals during the journey.

How often had his father described this journey! But the view was far more breathtaking than anyone could express in words. They climbed steadily upwards. Then the air began to get rarer and Debu felt his breath grow laboured.

'Tired, son?' Sonam Darka rode up alongside. He offered him a handful of gurpapri—roasted wheat flour mixed with dried fruit and lumps of coarse sugar. It was most welcome!

Debu smiled his thanks to the kindly Tibetan, who said, 'You need an occasional bite to keep you warm and energetic during the journey.' He rode on, droning a prayer under his breath. Debu wanted to ask what it meant but felt too shy.

After a while the track began to slope down again and by the evening they reached the meadow of Dung, where they camped for the night, next to the Gori river.

'Tomorrow we cross the passes, if there's no rain,' Kalyan Singh said, as they sat around the fire, drinking tea and eating the cold puris they had brought with them, with potatoes. 'Rain is dangerous,' he said shortly.

'Uncle,' Debu asked hesitantly. 'What was it like— that blizzard?' He had heard the story before, but he'd been in a state of shock then. Now, as he retraced his father's steps, he wanted to know it all.

Kalyan let out a deep breath. 'I've never faced anything like it,' he said, 'though I've been crossing these passes for forty years.' He gazed into the crackling fire. 'Usually the way back is easier, the climb to the passes is much gentler from the other side. But the sky was cloudy that morning. We should have waited another day . . . However, we were already late. There was the risk that the passes would get blocked if it snowed and we'd be stranded. So we decided to take the chance.'

'Who can foretell the vagaries of the weather?' Sonam Darka said, as he rotated his prayer wheel. 'I've seen ferocious blizzards blow up on an absolutely clear day.'

'It began to snow when we were halfway up to Kungri Bingri. By the time we got to the pass, we could hardly see a foot ahead of us.' Kalyan Singh paused. 'Your father had been ill, he was still quite weak. It was harder for him to keep up. We never even noticed

37

that he'd got left behind. We were all so taken up with our own struggle.'

Debu's eyes blurred. He could imagine it all—his father, normally so tough and fit, being buffeted by the snowy winds in his weakened state. Had he—had he really managed to make it to safety? Then the firelight glinted on the golden 'om' around Sonam Darka's neck and his heart lightened. The amulet was a sure sign of hope!

Sparks blew up as someone threw a few twigs in the fire. 'We managed to find a cave, took shelter under an overhanging rock,' Kalyan continued. 'We huddled close to the animals for warmth till the worst was over. It was only when we started again that we realized your father was missing. But we couldn't afford to go back and search. We had to cross the other two passes by the evening.'

'That's the worst thing about this route,' Sonam Darka said. 'You have to cross all three passes in one day. Not just the animals, we would freeze too if we tried to camp there.'

'But,' Debu said eagerly, 'Baujyu did manage to survive and even reach Gartok.'

'You'll find out yourself if he's alive,' Trilok sneered. Debu clenched his teeth. He had managed to maintain a distance from Cousin Trilok so far. Almost reflexively his hands went to the money-belt around his waist. Nobody had asked him again if he was carrying the silver coins; they'd been all caught up in their own affairs. But suddenly Debu noticed Trilok's gaze fixed on him. Had he noticed his gesture?

'That's what I've come here for,' he replied, struggling to keep his tone respectful. Then he stood up and patted his stomach again, trying to make the action look natural. 'I've eaten too much.'

'You won't find yourself saying that again too often,' Sonam Darka laughed. 'Better go to bed, boy. A tough day lies ahead tomorrow.' He touched Debu's arm lightly. The gesture cancelled out the hurt Trilok's words had inflicted.

The next morning, Sonam Darka shook him awake. 'Get up, Debu!' The sky was still dark and a biting wind blew. Sonam had brought him tea in his own silver-lined wooden bowl. Debu gulped it down gratefully with the usual sattu.

'We have to leave soon, son,' Sonam said. 'We cannot waste time.' Debu sprang out of his blanket and began to fold it up. Sonam's kindness energized him. Did he have a family, children, he wondered? But there was no room for further thought right now.

Men were rolling up tents, encouraging the animals to finish feeding. He patted Bijli, turned to give Jeevan a hand loading the sacks of provisions on the pack animals, then helped to put out the fires that had burned all night.

'Quick with that tent, Bijay!' Kalyan Singh yelled. 'Hurry up, Trilok, you can smoke later!'

When the ropes had been checked and tightened around the loads, the wooden saddles put on the horses and everyone had mounted, the caravan began to move.

The ascent began, a climb so steep that Debu could never have imagined it. He glanced up at the covering

39

of snow that fanned out towards them, and felt the chill numbing his cheeks. Despite the heaviness that weighted his head, the sense of awe was overpowering. He had never been so close to the high Himalayas before. And soon he would actually go over them!

Now Bijli's feet were sinking into the snow with each step, and Debu's heart contracted with anxiety as he scanned the whiteness, relieved only with clumps of dark rock poking out of it. But Bijli carried on as if it were one of their routine journeys.

They passed the Gori glacier and the first pass was before them—Unta Dhura, the camel's pass—17,590 feet high. Debu's heart lifted as they passed through the walls of snow. Everyone was silent, concentrating on the effort, except for the occasional baa from the sheep or a horse snorting, or a word of encouragement to the animals from the men. This pace had to be maintained. They pressed on to Jayanti Dhura, which lay to the east, slightly lower at 17,000 feet. Exhaustion began to slow them down, but they kept going. Debu glanced anxiously at the sky. The light was beginning to fade and they still had to reach Kungri Bingri, the last pass, and the highest, at 18,300 feet.

A sudden jolt tore him out of his reverie. Bijli had slipped. They were sliding down the rubble-strewn path! Chill fear knotted Debu's stomach. He clung to the pony, desperately whispering to her to hold on.

'Get off, Debu!' Sonam shouted, as Bijli dug in her heels and regained a shaky footing.

'Th's isn't child's play,' Trilok jibed, overtaking him

on the narrow trail. Debu's face reddened as he dismounted and trudged on.

Then his head jerked up. Someone was shouting, 'Careful, Trilok!' Debu turned to ice.

Cousin Trilok's horse was teetering at the edge of the trail! The ground was slipping away from beneath the horse's feet. There was a sickening crunch, and a hoarse cry forced itself from Trilok's throat. He tried to jump off. But one of his feet was caught in the stirrups! He shrieked, his arms reaching helplessly towards the mountainside as he fought to get free.

Sonam Darka, who was just ahead of Trilok, began to turn back. Trilok's horse was struggling to regain its footing—with no success. In another second, both the horse and the rider would tumble down the steep incline to certain death.

Shaking off the paralysis that gripped him, Debu ran and threw his arms around the horse's neck. Its front legs were still on firm ground. He tried to pull it back, tugging with all his might. It was like moving a huge rock, he could barely get a proper grip, but somehow he held on. The nervous animal shook its head violently, making it more difficult. If only he could hang on till the others came!

'Help! Save me!' Trilok screamed, his voice high-pitched with terror as he tried to disentangle his feet from the stirrups.

The men were shouting. What were they saying? Grimly Debu clung on. But the horse was sliding away—despite all his effort. Dragging him along too!

'Let go, Debu!' someone yelled. But how could he let the horse go plunging down the slope with Cousin Trilok?

'Debu! Let go!' Kalyan Singh commanded him. His heels were slipping through the snow, along with the horse. The animal's frightened neighing, together with Trilok's shrieks, added to his confusion. Should he let go and save himself?

No! Debu gave one last desperate heave and, miraculously, the horse jerked forward, almost falling on top of him. Someone pulled him away, just in time. It was Sonam Darka. Debu stood there panting, sweating despite the freezing cold. When he got his breath back, he whispered his thanks.

But they could not stop to talk or rest. They had to move on. Night was falling and the animals had not eaten the whole day. Debu could barely take note of the silent appreciation in everyone's eyes, register the pats on his back. He stumbled on ahead, an icy lump. Trilok's heavy wheezing was audible as they laboured on.

The whole party had dismounted. They did this whenever the climb got too stiff or the ground too slushy and slippery with melted snow. But the foul-tempered yaks and jibbos faced no problems. They negotiated the frosty paths and tricky climbs with ease.

The caravan was approaching the Kungri Bingri Pass when Kalyan Singh spoke at last. 'This is where we took refuge,' he said softly, riding up to Debu's side. He pointed to a huge rock jutting out of the mountainside, with a cave behind it. It was a natural shelter.

43

Debu tried to imagine the blizzard. This evening the sky was clear, with barely a few puffs of cloud dotting it. But the wind was biting cold. It chilled him even through his sheepskin coat, his close-fitting woollen trousers and the cap on his head. What had it been like, that other day, with the blinding whiteout obscuring everything?

Eagerly he looked around as they trudged on. What could he hope to find? A sign, a clue? A place where his father could have found refuge? There didn't seem any. Finally they crossed the pass, the fateful one. A low wall of stones marked the Indian boundary.

'We're in Tibet now,' Kalyan Singh said. Debu gazed around wonderingly.

INTO TIBET!

'There, there's Kang Rimpocche, holy Mount Kailash!' Sonam Darka exclaimed, folding his hands and raising them to his head. The others called out 'Jai Kailashpati!', hailing Lord Shiva, who was said to live on Kailash.

But Debu was so exhausted that his first sight of the fabled peak, sacred to both Buddhists and Hindus, failed to excite him. Sonam Darka dismounted near a large heap of stones, surrounded by a row of cloth flags, white and blue, yellow, green, red and black. Kalyan Singh gestured to Debu to do the same. Sonam added a stone and bowed. Then, one by one, so did Debu, along with the others.

'It's a laptche,' the Tibetan said in response to his questioning look. 'A religious monument. These flags are in our sacred colours. You will find many of them on the way.'

'They also serve as guides to travellers,' Bijay Singh added.

As they trotted down to Chirchin, their night camp, Debu noticed caves yawning out of the mountainside, visible in the starlight that softened the darkness. Could Baujyu have sheltered there?

'A holy man used to live here,' Sonam Darka said. 'He doesn't seem to be around today. We would have glimpsed the smoke from his fire.'

The terrible journey and the harrowing experience with Trilok's horse had drained them completely. It was an effort to set up camp and light the fires.

'You showed your mettle today, Debu!' Bijay Singh said, as they paused for breath after hammering in the tent stakes. He continued awkwardly, 'I know I said you were too young and inexperienced. You've proved me wrong.'

Debu tried to smile. 'I did what I had to,' he replied, embarrassed.

'I don't know about that,' Jeevan said. 'How many of us would have had the courage?'

The others grunted assent. A gush of pride warmed Debu and his exhaustion vanished. So did the nagging sense of hurt that Cousin Trilok hadn't bothered to utter a word of thanks, only thrown sullen glances at him.

Finally they settled down to their frugal meal and warmed their hands in the glowing embers. Stirring butter, flour and salt into the tea that was brewing in a long brass cylinder, Sonam Darka said, 'My son Nema could learn much from you. He's a little younger, a good boy, though still quite playful.'

'Do you have any other children, Uncle?' Debu asked, seizing this chance to satisfy his curiosity.

'Two daughters younger than Nema,' Sonam smiled. 'See—I bought these to set into headdresses for them.' He produced some large corals from a pocket. 'But I can see your eyes are closing. Go to bed, child,' he ended gently.

A strange thought flashed through Debu's mind. Could Sonam have been his father in a previous birth? It was extraordinary how he always sensed what Debu needed. Or maybe his mother . . . Fathers rarely pampered sons like that . . .

He woke up shivering to see Sonam Darka at the door of the tent.

'Oh, Uncle, you mustn't do this every day,' Debu protested, as he held out a bowl of tea.

Sonam smiled. 'Never mind, you will soon learn. It is important to rise early and make good use of the daylight.'

Debu nodded, ashamed that he'd overslept. 'When will we reach Gyanima?' he asked.

'On the eighth day, son,' Sonam said. He produced a fur-rimmed hat from his bag. 'Wear this,' he said. 'It'll protect you better than your cap.'

Debu accepted it diffidently. He didn't want to hurt Sonam's feelings by refusing, but felt a little shy putting it on. What would his fellow villagers say?

Luckily only Jeevan remarked. 'So, you've made

47

our little brother into a Tibetan, friend?' he guffawed. 'But you've done the right thing, Debu.'

Kalyan Singh nodded and Bijay Singh smiled as he twirled his moustache into points. A strong odour of perfume came from him. He carried attar in a silver case like a woman. The others teased him, but he didn't care.

Debu drew a deep breath to cool his excitement as he mounted Bijli. And the caravan set off again to the jingling of the animal's bells and the lilt of Jeevan's song.

After the gruelling crossing of the passes, the onward journey felt like a pleasure jaunt. Debu had never travelled on such a long stretch of level land before. The flat road, extending for miles without a single hill, felt strange. The grandeur of the distant snow-capped mountains was impressive, though. They rose, an amazing purple, almost melting into the sky. The ones closer were a dull brown, and the dust churned up by the animals' feet rose around them like smoke.

But when they camped in the open that night, he suddenly felt exposed and vulnerable.

To make things worse, Jeevan said, his eyes twinkling, 'Ho, Debu, do you know we might have to keep watch for robbers tonight? But you can handle a gun, can't you?'

'It's no joking matter,' Kalyan Singh said, reprovingly. 'All my goods were robbed once and I was lucky to save my life.'

However, the night passed peacefully, as did the others on their way to Gyanima. The sun blazed down during the day, even though a strong wind blew constantly. Debu's eyes smarted from the glare that bounced off the white ground. He was thankful for the hat Sonam Darka had given him, because it shaded his eyes well. The road was comfortable for the animals— quite wide in some places and free of stones. But there was little water to be found and they had to take care to fill up whenever they found a stream. Luckily there was some grass, sparse though it was. So Bijli didn't go hungry. Laptches dotted the road, some so large that they could be glimpsed from far, as well as chortens or the tombs of lamas.

As they stopped at a laptche to add stones as their offering, Debu noticed one that had words inscribed on it. Curious, he picked it up.

'It's a holy mantra, a prayer to Chenrezig, the Buddha of Compassion,' Sonam Darka told him. '*Om mani padme hum . . .*' he chanted. 'It means, "Hail the jewel in the lotus".'

'Oh . . . that's what you have been repeating all this time!' Debu exclaimed.

AT GYANIMA

The caravan pushed on ahead and after a while a large structure loomed into view.

'That's the fort of Gyanima!' Jeevan pointed out.

'Have we reached?' Debu asked eagerly.

'No,' Sonam laughed. 'The fort is visible from a great distance because the air is so clear.'

It was a formidable sight, though in ruins, as Debu realized when they came closer. Imagine, I'm actually arriving at a Tibetan trading town, he thought, tingling with anticipation. Then his heart leapt, suddenly. His father might be right here in Gyanima! The traders' annual visit took place around the same time each year. Baujyu might be waiting to rejoin his companions.

But he hugged this hope to himself, not caring to deal with the others' scepticism.

'This is the biggest trade mart of western Tibet,' Sonam Darka told him. 'You can get almost anything here.'

'I can well believe it.' Debu gazed wide-eyed at the spreading forest of tents—of all hues, sizes and shapes.

'The aristocratic-looking white tents, with patterns across the doorway, belong to the Lhasa merchants,' Sonam said. 'Dokpa nomads have put up the black yak hair ones.'

'And the small, plain tents, without prayer flags hung in front, belong to Shaukas like us,' Kalyan Singh added.

'If it's the biggest trading mart,' Debu asked, puzzled, 'why aren't there any houses?'

'The Tarjun, the official in charge of this area, forbids it,' Kalyan Singh explained. 'We wanted to build shacks to store our goods, but he refused. He said the spirits of the ground must not be disturbed.'

'The spirits are more potent in some parts,' Sonam Darka said, nodding.

The day was dying and the wind turned as sharp as a knife. On the way they passed some women carrying long baskets on their backs. Their plaited hair was wound around their heads, covered with bright headcloths and bells hung from their waists. Debu gazed curiously at the striped aprons they wore on top of their long robes, and the numerous bead necklaces around their necks and wrists.

They found a camping site and began to settle in. Putting up the tents was a daunting task. The strong wind kept defeating their efforts. They had to weight the flaps with large stones to keep it out.

51

'*Phew!*' Debu wrinkled his nose as a strong odour rose from the mixture of juniper wood and animal dung Jeevan was setting ablaze.

'Now you know why brother Bijay carries his perfumes,' Jeevan winked. 'This is the only fuel available here.'

'Well, I'm glad to have something to warm myself!'
Kalyan Singh frowned.

The heat was certainly welcome, though they had
to stick to their travel fare of barley flour and tea
instead of the more exciting meal Debu had hoped
for. It was impossible to cook on the wavering flames
of the fire, nor was anything tastier available.

Debu slept well that night, despite the fact that the
ground was freezing and they had to use extra
bedding. He felt safe here, after camping in the open
countryside.

Today, today I will find Baujyu, he exulted
as he awoke the next morning. Eagerly, he
led Bijli out to graze in the marshy land,
which surrounded the area. She
suddenly lifted her head,

neighed happily and broke into a gallop, jerking the reins out of his hand.

'Bijli! Bij-li!' Debu cried, running after her. But she was already cropping greedily on the fresh green grass!

'Oh, well at least someone's getting decent food,' he laughed wryly. 'Have your fill, Bijli,' he murmured. 'Do you know you're visiting your native land?' Bijli stopped munching as if she were listening attentively and nodded as if she'd understood!

It was wonderful—after the monotony of the march—to be amongst people again. People from so many different places, with so much diversity in dress, appearance and speech, so much to sell and exchange. The tall, fair-complexioned men with aquiline features wearing fur hats were Kashmiris, Bijay Singh told him. They were selling silk, exquisitely fine pashmina shawls and saffron. Debu found their speech strange and different. The traders from Ladakh, with their long pigtails, could hardly be distinguished from the Tibetans. Their produce was similar to the Kashmiris and they also sold dried apricots, which were much in demand. Kalyan Singh picked up a stock for their party since they made an excellent snack. The Tibetan officials were grand in colourful silk; their women sported silver tiaras studded with gems and long necklaces of coral.

'Oh, Ma! What long hair!' Debu exclaimed, gazing at a woman whose numerous braids swept to the ground behind her skirt.

Sonam guffawed heartily. 'It's not all her hair,' he said. 'It's been plaited into strings and attached to long ribbons. She's a Dokpa.'

Jeevan laughed too. 'Maybe we should tell the girls in our village about this style.'

Debu smiled. Some rough-looking men with wild hair accompanied the woman, dressed in fur-lined coats. With one naked arm slipped out of their sleeves, they seemed unperturbed by the chilly wind blowing on their bare chests. Jeevan went up to check the borax they were selling, another item the traders carried back to India.

Then a group of men and women, mounted on large, splendid horses, dashed up. As they got off, Debu noticed that these women had floor-length braids too, but ornamented profusely with silver coins.

'How many rupees do you think they are carrying, eh?' Jeevan nudged him.

'It would be hard to tell,' Debu grinned. 'Are they Dokpas too? They look different.'

The tall, broad-shouldered men were armed with both rifles and swords and wore short, roomy sheepskin coats. Broad-brimmed hats crowned their heads and they sported leather boots with pointed toes on their feet. But Debu was fascinated by the ornate scabbards at their waists, studded with gold, turquoise and coral.

'They're Khampas,' Sonam said. 'They own large herds of cattle and come here to trade wool from their sheep and goats, salt and gold as well.'

'There'll be so much to tell Hayat,' Debu said, gazing at them wonderstruck.

But the day, which began so well, turned out to be cruelly disappointing. Debu was shocked to discover that Dawa Nangal had died the year before and no one knew where his son was.

'Don't worry,' Jeevan said. 'You can sell your goods through my partner.'

Debu thanked him, but this setback was bitter. He cheered up somewhat when he got good value for his cloth and decided to use the money to buy some wool to take back.

'Don't sell everything here,' Kalyan Singh advised. 'Save some goods to trade in Gartok. You might get a better price there.'

'Thanks for the suggestion, Uncle,' Debu said. 'I don't have too much to sell, but still—' He stopped, thinking of his tankas. Should he ask Kalyan Singh to help him dispose of them? Something made him hesitate. Though Trilok had kept his distance, Debu had noticed the man gazing at him suspiciously several times. Perhaps he should sell them and get rid of the burden. But maybe it would be better to let his father take the responsibility when he found him.

So he concentrated on making enquiries from the Tibetan traders, if any of them knew anything about his father. But over and over again, he got the same answer—'No'. Still, he continued to ask, even though his fund of hope was beginning to dwindle.

Soon the week they spent in Gyanima became a trial. Debu was desperate to push on to Gartok. But he could only go ahead when everyone else was ready to.

At last the day came. 'How long will it take to

reach Gartok?' Debu asked Sonam Darka as he trotted beside him.

'A march of eight to ten days,' he replied, adding, 'We're travelling on the jonglam, the great road that leads to Lhasa.'

Lhasa! Despite Debu's preoccupation, the name sent ripples of excitement down his back. How he would have liked to visit the fabled city! He knew that the Dalai Lama lived there in the magnificent Potala palace.

Perhaps I will, some day, he thought, examining the barren tableland that surrounded them. There was scarcely a tree to be seen. If it hadn't been for the frequent laptches marking the trail they might well have lost their way.

Then he exclaimed in surprise. A lone horseman hurtled past at top speed, lines of weariness etched on his face. Two other horses galloped alongside him. 'Why's he in such a hurry?' Debu asked Sonam Darka.

'He's carrying some urgent official message,' the tall man smiled. 'He cannot stop except to eat or change horses—not even to sleep. The breast fastening of his overcoat is sealed with wax and the official mark stamped on it, so he cannot take off his clothes. It can only be broken by the official in charge when it's delivered.'

'He'll have to ride day and night, isn't it?' Bijay Singh asked. 'And if he stops he'll be severely punished.'

Sonam nodded.

'What a difficult job!' Debu said, turning to look at the man who was already far away.

By nightfall they reached a resting place and made a welcome halt. There were several of them on this route, every twenty to seventy miles either houses made of sun-dried brick or large tents provided shelter to weary travellers.

Gartok was just a couple of days away when they camped at a small settlement. Close by was a monastery.

'Let's pay our respects to the Lama,' Sonam Darka said, after they were settled for the evening.

Debu had heard about the amazing powers of the lamas. Their ability to read minds, predict the future, perform magic feats, even fly and change shape. I can ask the Lama if he knows where my father is, he thought. Eagerly he swung himself onto Bijli's back.

THE LAMA

T he monastery was a cluster of buildings surrounded
by a wall, clinging to the slope of a hill. Built of
sun-dried bricks, the ends of its wooden roofs turned
upwards. Two fierce-looking statues of lions guarded
the gates. Debu entered with mingled hope and curiosity.

'We always pay our respects to the lamas,' Kalyan
Singh whispered. 'They are extremely powerful. We
take care not to displease them.'

But Debu was busy taking in new sights. The
monastery was unlike any place of worship he had
ever seen before. Prayer cylinders, flags and yaks' tails
were placed here and there. They walked down the
courtyard into a veranda with a large cloth frill running
around the roof. It had red pillars, and an ornate prayer
wheel taller than Debu himself. Sonam spun it, then
folded his hands, raised them to his head and prostrated

himself on the ground. They followed suit, and then entered through a multi-coloured door with bright strips of cloth hung over it. The scent of burning incense and butter lamps was the same as in temples back home. He could hear a regular droning sound coming from inside, along with the sound of gongs.

'It's the monks chanting their prayers,' Sonam Darka said.

Debu entered the dark audience chamber hesitantly, overawed by the presence of the shaven-headed monks in yellow robes, the darkly gleaming images lit by rows and rows of lamps. The all-merciful Buddha was seated in the centre surrounded with other deities. One of them captured Debu's gaze. She had many arms like the Hindu goddess Kali, and was slaying a demon. There were hand bells too like the ones they used in worship.

His eyes rose to the walls painted with scenes from the Buddha's life, then his thoughts pulled him back.

Could he dare to ask the Lama about his father? Suddenly he went cold. His father had told him that they always offered gifts to the lamas—and . . . he hadn't brought anything! Suppose the Lama felt slighted, got annoyed? Debu tried to fall back and disappear in the group.

'Come forward,' Kalyan Singh whispered, tugging at his elbow. 'See that's him, the Head Lama of this monastery.'

Debu looked up nervously. He blinked in surprise, the yellow-clad figure seated on the gilded throne was a boy! A boy even younger than he was—maybe as old as Hayat—with a round, chubby face! A tall man wearing silk robes stood near him.

He recollected what he had heard. It was believed that when a lama died, he was reborn soon after. The senior lamas of the monastery would search for the baby who would be his successor. Various signs and tests helped them to prove that he was the right one. That's why some lamas were young children.

Debu saw all the others bowing respectfully and did the same. Perhaps this lama might overlook the fact that he hadn't brought him a gift. But as he bent low, the top in his pocket, the one Hayat had given him, rolled out.

Debu froze, then grabbed the top. But when he glanced up apologetically, he saw the little Lama's black eyes glittering with excitement. Immediately, he picked up the top and offered it to him. The Lama flashed him a delighted smile. Debu bowed again and stepped back, relieved. After that, the others presented the Lama with strips of silk, dried fruit and sweets.

The Lama blessed them, very seriously, and a monk placed strips of silk around their necks and gave Kalyan Singh a leather pouch containing butter. Then he poured tea from a silver kettle into the cups they carried in their waist-bags.

The Lama said politely in his fluty voice, 'Is all well in your country? Is your ruler well?'

Kalyan Singh replied on their behalf in the affirmative.

As Debu sipped the salted butter tea, he wondered

if he should ask about his father. Then he dismissed the thought. The Lama's questions seemed routine. He didn't want to make things awkward by asking questions for which there might be no answers.

Debu turned to have a last glimpse of the monastery as they left. Waves of sonorous sound swept the air as the monks began to play the trumpets in homage to the setting sun. Its rays lit up the gilded roof dramatically.

'The Lama seemed pleased with your gift,' Sonam Darka smiled. 'That tall man was his father, you know,' he added.

'Wh't else w'ld a child be h'ppy with?' Trilok Singh burst out scornfully.

He's back to being his normal mean self, Debu thought. Ever since he had nearly fallen off the mountain, Trilok had been quiet and withdrawn. He had kept his distance from Debu, though Debu had noticed him turn a surly eye on him now and again.

'He is no ordinary child,' Kalyan Singh said, with a warning frown. 'He is a Lama.' He turned to Debu. 'I was going to hand you a scarf to give him. It struck me just then that you may not have brought anything.'

Trilok Singh snorted and Debu saw Sonam's face redden with anger.

Sonam was about to say something when Kalyan Singh spoke. 'First, you behaved foolishly on the way to the pass and endangered others' lives. And now you are being disrespectful.' He went on, 'We have always honoured the lamas, worshipped the Buddha and been rewarded with his blessings.'

'Yes,' Jeevan added. 'You will bring bad luck to us with this behaviour.'

.'I'll say what I want,' Trilok said defiantly and stomped off.

The others gazed after him, anxious frowns wrinkling their brows.

Debu found it hard to sleep that night. Questions crowded his mind. They would be in Gartok soon. Suppose he couldn't trace his father? No, no, he squashed down the thought. I definitely will. The moneybag felt like a lump of iron digging into his belly as he tossed and turned. It felt so uncomfortable that he decided to untie it and place it under the rolled-up old shawl that was his pillow.

Perhaps the same restlessness made him come awake in the middle of the night. No, it was something pressing on his chest, almost suffocating him. A terrifying thought coursed through his mind. Was it a robber? He could hear a jagged, repetitive sound— someone breathing heavily close by. But he had heard that robbers never came silently. They let out fierce cries to terrorize their prey and fired their guns. Could it be a wild animal then? Should he cry out for help?

He was about to scream when he felt hands move down his chest towards his waist. And recognized that nauseous smell! Quick as a flash, Debu reached out and grabbed the searching hands. He heard a strangled exclamation. The hands fought frantically to free themselves. Debu struggled to hold on. But the hands were fiendishly strong. Sluggish with sleep, Debu could not grip them hard enough and they wrenched themselves out of his grasp. With a muffled cry he sat up and flung off his bedclothes. Someone was stumbling away!

He was about to cry out, give chase, when something stopped him. It would lead to more quarrels, could even delay their departure. Debu lay down again, and thanked providence for the impulse that had made him remove the moneybag. He would have to be very, very careful now.

AN UNEXPECTED HAPPENING

The sun almost blinded Debu when he stepped out of his tent the next day. And as he gulped down his breakfast, Jeevan remarked, 'We'll have to be careful that our cakes of jaggery don't melt away. It's one of those days.'

Kalyan Singh drew away from his hookah to glance at the cloudless sky. 'We'd better leave right away,' he said.

'Jaggery melting?' Debu asked. Jaggery was hard, and it melted only when it was exposed to direct heat.

Jeevan smiled. 'The sun gets so hot here sometimes that it melts.'

Just then Bijay Singh asked, 'Was there an animal prowling in the tent last night? I heard weird sounds. I almost got up to investigate, when they stopped.'

Debu started. He flung a surreptitious glance at Trilok who sat sullenly by himself in a corner, chewing at a piece of dried meat.

'Better check your belongings,' Jeevan laughed and winked. 'It could have been an animal who likes the taste of money.'

Trilok's brow darkened. He pulled out a bottle from his bag and tipped some of the liquid into his cup and gulped it down.

Sonam Darka, who was fingering his prayer beads, frowned. Jeevan said, 'Brother, it's better to stay off the chhang. It'll be a long day in the saddle and you might just tumble off your horse. And who knows, we may not even notice, if you remain in the rear, as you usually like to.'

They were all off-guard, bent over with laughter, when Trilok hurled himself at Jeevan.

Kalyan Singh started up, shouting, 'Stop that! Stop it at once!'

'Enough, stop it!' The others ran to separate them.

Debu's heart thumped sickeningly. He was thankful now that he'd held his tongue the night before.

It took a determined effort by Sonam, Bijay and other members of the group to tear them apart.

'I was only joking,' Jeevan said aggrievedly.

'You had better behave yourself at Gartok, Trilok,' Kalyan Singh glared at him. 'Else I'll hand you over to the Tibetan authorities.'

Trilok paled beneath his stubble. It was an extreme step Kalyan Singh was threatening him with. He might have to pay a heavy fine, or worse, be given a severe beating. He turned away without a word and began to tend to his jibbo.

It was a bad beginning to the day. All the same, Debu could never have dreamt what lay in store for him. The preparations to leave were complete, and he was about to mount Bijli when the sound of hoof beats exploded in his ears.

It was a horseman, a Tibetan. 'Stop!' he cried, reining up with a jerk. The whole group turned around startled. Trilok looked positively terrified.

Debu gazed at the man bewildered. Had Trilok done something wrong?

'What's the matter?' Sonam Darka asked. 'What do you want from us?'

'I have come from the monastery,' the man said imperiously. 'The Lama has asked for him. The rest of you are free to go on.' He gestured towards Debu.

'Me? But why?' Debu gazed at him stunned.

Kalyan Singh looked equally surprised. But he recovered fast. 'What has the boy done?' he asked in a low, courteous voice. 'If he has displeased the Lama in any way, please let him know I apologize on his behalf and am prepared to offer any kind of compensation.'

'What compensation can you give the Lama?' the man said scornfully. 'He just wants the boy to stay behind.'

'But I can't!' Debu cried. 'I have to look for my father.'

The man frowned ominously. His hard narrow eyes sliced through Debu as he said, 'The Lama wants it. You will have to stay.'

67

Kalyan Singh tugged at his moustache, distressed. The others exchanged troubled looks.

Then Sonam Darka touched Debu gently on his shoulder. In a low tone he said, 'It is a great honour, son.' Debu got the hint of a warning.

Kalyan Singh drew Debu aside. 'If you refuse, it could create problems,' he whispered.

Debu's heart sank. Tears stung his eyes. How could he stay on in the monastery and abandon his quest?

'We'll search for your father in Gartok,' Sonam Darka placed a comforting arm around his shoulders. 'Don't worry, son, everything will turn out all right.' Debu gazed helplessly into his friend's eyes. He had begun to think of Sonam as a link to his father. And now it was being broken.

'Yes, Debu,' Kalyan Singh added. 'I promise. I'll even dispose of the rest of your merchandise and keep the money for you. And . . .' he said softly, 'we'll try to persuade the Lama to let us take you back on our return journey. I'll approach the Jongpen, if necessary.'

An impulse led Debu to whisper, 'Uncle, can I give you these tankas for safekeeping? You can sell them, perhaps. There are two hundred.'

Kalyan Singh narrowed his eyes, then nodded.

Debu turned his back to the group and quickly passed the moneybag to Kalyan, who hid it in his voluminous coat.

Then dejectedly, he gathered up his belongings and followed the horseman on Bijli. She seemed to have sensed his mood and dragged her steps. He could not help casting a last desperate glance at the caravan as he left. His companions stood there with sympathetic looks on their faces, Trilok stood a little apart from the others, as usual. Sonam Darka raised his hand but he could only manage a feeble wave in reply.

'Come along,' said the man sharply.

Debu followed him gloomily.

As they approached the monastery, the sound of cymbals and the long Tibetan trumpets came to his ears, along with the beating of drums and chanting of '*Om mani padme hum*'.

But instead of yesterday's excitement, fear crawled over Debu's arms. Why had the Lama asked him to stay back? Did he want him to become a monk? Would he never see his family again?

They passed through the gates. 'Wait here,' the man said gruffly. 'And don't try to go anywhere! I'm taking your pony to the stables.'

Debu clenched his fists, trying to keep calm as he waited in the large entrance hall. The gaudy colours of the bright silk thangkas hanging on the walls clashed in his head, making it ache. The demon faces and skulls on them stared at him menacingly; the smell of incense and rancid butter was suffocating . . .

And then, his eye fell on a large image of the Buddha set in an alcove. How serene he looked! As Debu gazed at it, he remembered that the Buddha had preached peace and was infinitely merciful.

So, when the summons came, he faced the Lama calmly. A broad smile lit the boy's round, rosy face when he set eyes on Debu. 'Sit,' he said, in his fluty voice.

'Boy,' said the Lama's father, 'the Lama wishes to make you his special friend.'

Debu blinked. Was that all? He would have loved to be the Lama's friend, but right now he had a goal, which he could not abandon for anything.

Luckily, he remembered to bow low and say, 'I am deeply honoured.'

Still smiling, the little Lama produced the top and held it out to him. Debu was suddenly reminded of Hayat. He took the top and bent to spin it expertly on the ground. The Lama clapped with delight, then spun it himself. Impulsively Debu picked it up and showed him all the tricks that had delighted Hayat so much. The Lama clapped again, then beckoned to his father, who produced a set of marbles made of semi-precious stones. 'Let's play,' he said.

Debu nodded and the Lama skipped down to the courtyard, his entourage following. Debu glanced around surreptitiously. Where had they stabled Bijli? If only he could find out! The caravan could not have gone too far. If he and Bijli travelled fast, there was a chance they could still catch up with them. And if they had gone beyond the Lama's territory they did not need to fear.

But as he squatted on the ground to play marbles with the Lama, he knew it was useless. Surrounded with people as he was, there wasn't a whisker of a chance to escape. He would have to bide his time.

At noon, the Lama's father came and said, 'Lobsang, it's time for your prayers.' Debu's heart leapt. Maybe now!

His hopes were dashed to the ground when Lobsang said, 'Come along with me.' Reluctantly he followed and sat quietly, hands folded, amongst the rows of monks chanting their prayers, swaying back and forth.

After that it was time for Lobsang's lessons. Now, Debu thought, now's my chance. But one of the monks was left with him, for company, as they said. Debu had to smile, though he could have wept. The caravan must have progressed so far by now that he could never hope to catch up.

The monk was a jolly and talkative man, with a huge, discoloured lump on his forehead. He began to question Debu about his life back home. Debu answered mechanically, his mind in a whirl. How could he get rid of the monk? He racked his brains frantically. When the idea came, it was so simple that it made him smile. The monk smiled back and nodded.

'This thing on your forehead,' Debu began, 'my father had one too.'

'Oh,' the monk fingered it, his smile growing fixed.

'He got rid of it,' Debu continued.

'How?' the monk asked eagerly.

'A holy man told him a way.' Debu pretended to concentrate. 'Yes . . . you have to touch it with three things and repeat a mantra.'

'What three things?' the monk asked eagerly. 'Do you remember the mantra?'

'Hmmm . . . I think . . . a piece of silver dipped in the butter of a holy lamp, a lump of salt and a few grains of rice. And—' he paused, feeling ashamed . . . the man looked so trusting . . . but he had to get away!

71

'I remember the mantra, it's the one I chant to keep evil spirits away at night.'

The monk looked around, then whispered, 'If I bring those three things, will you tell me the mantra?'

'Of course,' Debu said.

As he had expected, the man got up and hurried off.

Debu dashed out through the entrance hall right away. Where could the stables be? His eyes fell on a door that opened on the left side of the courtyard. But it led only into a dark rectangular room. Debu paused, confused. Anxiously, he searched for another door. Then a sound made him halt—someone humming under his breath. He held his breath and flattened himself against the wall, thankful the rooms were so badly lit. A monk passed by without even a glance in his direction.

Debu's heart vaulted up. He had found a way out! The door through which the monk had entered. It was hidden beneath a large silk hanging.

A set of ladder-like stairs led down from it, into the open. Debu scrambled down, then stopped to take stock. He had to hurry; they must already be hunting for him. Like an answer to a prayer, a gust of wind brought a whiff of horse dung. He was close! He glanced about desperately.

Then he saw them, the row of buildings to his left. The stacks of hay piled outside and the scattered horse dung made it obvious. He ran, ducking through a low doorway, and found himself in the monastery's stables.

It was easy to locate his beloved Bijli, who let out a welcoming neigh. Debu's eyes scanned the walls for his wooden saddle. He was just taking it down when the sound of a heavy footstep made his heart thump. He dropped to the ground and began to creep along the wall behind the horses. But as he crouched in the smelly straw, a muttered oath rang in his ear and a hard hand came down with painful force on his shoulder.

'What are you doing here?' It was the man who had brought him to the monastery. He jerked Debu roughly to his feet and glared at him. 'Trying to run away—hunh?'

The monks let out high-pitched cries of condemnation as Debu was led before the Lama. Debu kept his head down and tried to fight his anger and despair.

Lobsang looked sad as Debu stood before him, flushed and defiant. 'I thought you liked being my friend,' he said.

Debu softened. He had expected outrage, punishment, had been bracing himself for it. But Lobsang's words puzzled him. Then a thought sprang into his mind. What if he told him why he was trying to escape?

So he swallowed hard and said, 'I—I do like being your friend. I liked playing with you . . . because I have a younger brother just your age. But—'

'But what?' Lobsang's father asked sternly.

Debu blurted it all out, his father getting lost in the

blizzard, the discovery of the amulet, and his quest. How he had left his mother and brother all alone and pleaded to join the expedition.

'I was desperate to go on, continue my search!' he cried. 'Otherwise I would have been too happy to stay here as long as you liked.'

There was a long pause. Lobsang's babyish face looked troubled. Debu glanced surreptitiously at his father. Something told him the final decision would be his.

Quickly he prostrated himself, 'I know you are as merciful as the Buddha. I beg you to let me continue my search.'

A sudden exclamation made him start up. It was one of the monks. 'A trader lost in a blizzard?'

Debu nodded eagerly. 'I heard something about a man being saved by a lama from the Darcchen monastery,' the monk said frowning. 'From somewhere near the Kungri Bingri Pass . . .'

'You did!' Debu leapt up.

'Yes,' the monk said. 'The lama had been meditating in one of the caves and he found the man half-dead outside . . . I heard.'

Debu threw an appealing glance at Lobsang, who seemed lost in thought.

'How can I find that lama?' he asked breathlessly.

'Darcchen is not too far from here, isn't it?' Lobsang said, turning to his father.

The tall man nodded. His voice was kind as he said, 'We can send you there with an escort.'

'Thank you! Oh thank you!' Debu cried.

Then he heard the monk clearing his throat. 'I'm not sure if the man survived,' he said. 'I heard he was very, very ill.'

Debu's excitement ebbed right away. Then he took a deep breath. 'In any case,' he said slowly. 'I must find out.'

Lobsang nodded sympathetically, his face full of an understanding beyond his years.

'I will pray that you find your father in good health and return to your country without any difficulty,' he said solemnly.

Debu bowed low in gratitude.

ON THE ROAD AGAIN

'May the gracious Buddha watch over you,' Lobsang said. Debu bowed.

Morning had come and his excitement was bubbling over as he stood before Lobsang to bid him farewell. The little Lama produced a talisman, a turquoise mounted in silver. 'Wear this around your neck,' he said. 'It will bring you luck.'

Debu bent his head to receive it. It was believed that turquoise protected the wearer from the evil eye. As he rode away, he wondered if he would ever meet Lobsang again.

Debu had an escort of three—Tenzen the glum, aloof fellow who'd brought him to the monastery, and two others. Showing great generosity, Lobsang also sent a yak laden with provisions and gifts for Debu along with them.

The trail was dreary and monotonous. But the monk's story about the rescued man had buoyed him up him so much that Debu felt he could fly there!

'Can we make it in one day, if we go very fast?' he asked Tenzen.

The dour horseman curled his lip and shook his head. 'Not possible,' he said. 'Too far.'

Debu tried to clamp down his impatience. But his thoughts kept weaving back and forth like a crazy pendulum. Would he really find his father at Darcchen? Or would the others find him at Gartok? How would they all connect?

To calm himself, he began to repeat the Gayatri mantra. It meant, 'May the Almighty God illuminate our minds to lead us along the righteous path.' His mother had told him that it was a very powerful prayer and that Lord Brahma had conceived it before he created the world. The rhythm of the Sanskrit words soothed him as he recited them and the monotonous journey seemed less tiresome.

Slowly, the day progressed. The sun lost its heat and darkness gathered. Before night fell, they set up their camp by the roadside. Luckily the other two men relaxed and opened up now, though Tenzen remained sour and distant. So dinner was a comparatively cheery affair, under the amazingly bright stars that twinkled out of a clear sky.

Tomorrow we'll reach the monastery! All keyed up, Debu pulled the blankets over himself. I'll meet the man who saved Baujyu. The thought excited him so much that despite his exhaustion he found it hard to fall asleep.

He had barely dozed off when he awoke with a start—choking and gasping. Something was pressing down on him—something heavy and suffocating! He struggled to throw it off but it kept falling back. Was he dreaming, reliving that other night's incident? No, it was real! Panic-stricken, Debu was about to shout for help when he heard a peculiar high-pitched cry, 'Ullu-llu-llu-uu!' Instantly, he froze with terror. He knew what that cry meant, his father had told him, even imitated it for him.

Robbers!

Debu thrashed about madly, trying to get the throttling mass off his head. He realized what the robbers had done. They had cut the tent ropes! It was one of their tricks—to prevent their victims from resisting. But he had to escape! Fighting for breath, he wriggled out somehow. The unnerving cries were punctuated by the sound of horses whinnying in fear, and the rat-a-tat-tat of guns.

He burst out into the cold, clear starlight to see three horses galloping away, with riders on their backs. They were pulling a fourth one along. Bijli, he thought with horror, watching her struggle to throw off her reins. If only he'd been quicker!

Bang! A gun went off, right behind him, almost deafening him. It was a rough-looking man—a robber—chasing the horsemen, firing at them. He realized with a shock that it was the men from the monastery who were running away with Bijli.

'Follow them! Don't let them get away!' someone yelled. As if they had heard, one of the horsemen turned and fired back and the robber fell off his mount shrieking with pain.

A helpless rage overpowered him. How could they abandon him and take his horse, too? The Lama had sent them along for his protection! He was about to run after them when a hard hand grabbed him and jerked him around. He found himself staring into a fierce face with eyes like slits and a cruel mouth with a jagged scar beneath it, framed by a head of shaggy hair. 'It's a boy!' The man thrust him away so violently that he fell.

'This is all there is.' One of the robbers dragged the yak to the wild man and showed him the bags of provisions, while Debu staggered to his feet. The robbers tore at the bags, then flung them down in disgust.

'Only food! Are you sure this is all?'

'Search yourself then. You can see there's only one tent and no other pack animals.'

The wild man swore. 'Paupers!' he spat. 'Just our wretched luck that we couldn't find anything better.' He turned to Debu. 'Search him,' he ordered. 'He might be hiding something in his clothes.'

Before Debu could protest, the robber dragged Debu's coat off, then the cotton shirt he wore beneath it. Soon all his clothes lay in a heap next to him, while he stood there naked in the bitter cold, his teeth chattering so hard that he was afraid they'd fall out. Despite his misery, he could not help feeling thankful that he'd given the tankas to Kalyan Singh. The robbers could only find the few coins he kept for emergencies on him. The next minute he was not too sure, though.

'Let's finish him off,' the robber who had searched him suggested, a short man with a pinched, mean face. 'He's no use to us. If we keep him, it'll be another mouth to feed.'

'No, wait,' said the wild-looking man. From his commanding tone, Debu guessed that he was the leader. He grabbed the heavy gold rings Debu wore in his ears. 'He's a Shauka,' he said, grinning evilly. 'Probably the son of a trader. Maybe we can get something out of him!'

'What will you get?' the other man scoffed. 'His father has abandoned him and run off.'

'No,' Debu cried out, stung. 'My father's at Gartok. I had stopped at the monastery for the day. Those men were escorting me to Gartok.'

Desperately, he searched their faces for a reaction.

'Stayed back at the monastery? What for?' The robber chief frowned distrustfully.

'Because the Lama had taken a liking to me.' Their confused looks encouraged him to continue, 'See, he gave me this lucky talisman.' He lifted up the turquoise charm for their benefit.

'Much luck it has brought you!' One of the robbers laughed.

'Quiet!' The robber chieftain barked. 'Maybe he's meant to share the luck with us. Come along, boy,' he said briskly. 'Put on your clothes. Get up behind me on my horse. And you, Chumbel, pick up those bags. We can make use of the food at least!' A young, fresh-faced robber ran to do his bidding.

Miserably, Debu hoisted himself up behind the robber chief, then almost fainted from the stench that came from him—a mixture of ancient sweat, badly cured leather, rancid butter and, of course, chhang. Why did this have to happen, he thought, just when he was going to find out something about his father? And what lay in store for him with the robbers?

THE ROBBERS' CAMP

A bitter-cold dawn was breaking as Debu arrived at the robbers' camp. It was just a clump of rough black yak hair tents, hidden behind a hillock. A meagre flock of sheep milled about in a small enclosure next to it. Two men, who'd apparently been left behind to guard the camp, ran to greet them eagerly.

But their faces dropped when the others told them, cursing, what a failure the raid had been. They flung curious, hostile glances at Debu.

Debu alighted and stood there uncertainly, wondering what would happen next.

'Here, Chumbel! Take my horse!' the robber chief shouted. Debu looked at him expectantly, but the chief strode off, ignoring him.

The two men got busy, lighting a fire of juniper twigs, then set water to boil on it. Debu crept away to huddle in a corner. Surreptitiously, he gazed at the wide flat expanse around him. Was there any chance of getting away? But he wouldn't know which way to go. Maybe he should have listened to his elders and stayed home. Maybe he was not destined to find his father, he thought, rubbing his sleeve across his eyes.

An ear-splitting shout shattered his reverie. It was the robbers calling out to him. He rose and shuffled up to them, full of dread. But they just wanted to give him some of the hot butter tea they were drinking, along with a small portion of barley flour. Debu's bones ached, and his ears felt sore where his earrings had been torn off. But as the warmth of the tea coursed through his body, his spirits lifted somewhat. Maybe he could convince the robbers that it was in their interest to take good care of him and return him to his father.

As Debu was drinking his tea, the robbers all vanished into one of the tents. He could hear agitated talk coming from it. Was that the chief's tent? It was in slightly better shape than the others, there was even a bit of ornamentation on the door flap. The voices suddenly grew louder. What were they talking about? Just then the door flap was flung open and the mean-faced man came out. Debu's heart darted up like a terrified bird. The man strode up to him and dragged him to his feet. 'Come along,' he said.

Something about the way he tugged at his arm stung Debu. Almost in reflex, he pushed him away. The robber's face turned purple and he slapped Debu viciously across his face.

'Insolent pup!' The man pulled at him so hard that he almost fell. Somehow he staggered into the robber chief's tent.

The chief was seated on a rug, something like the ones his mother wove, leaning against a bolster with a similar woollen covering. But grime and dust had dimmed the original colours so that the pattern was barely visible. A huge grey dog that sat by him growled menacingly. Debu jumped, almost catching his tongue between his teeth. It was not a dog but a wolf!

'He's a bad-tempered fellow,' his escort growled. 'He pushed me away when I was fetching him.'

The robber chief's high-pitched laugh rang out. The wolf stared at him confused, and swished his tail briefly.

'So, the puppy has spirit. Obviously he doesn't like you, Dingmo.' He guffawed again. 'Tell us, boy,' he went on, taking a deep draught from his cup of chhang. 'Where's your father trading? Gyanima or Gartok? What goods has he brought to sell? Tell me quickly or . . .' He paused and grinned again. 'Do you remember what this friend of ours wanted to do? If you're no use to us—we'll have no choice.'

'Come on! Out with it!' Dingmo snarled. 'Or we'll set the wolf on you!'

'Neither . . . I mean, I don't know,' Debu stammered, as a clammy sweat chilled his brow. Would they actually try to find his father and ask for ransom? Or was it a trick to follow the caravan and loot it?

'Don't get too clever with me! You said he was at Gartok!' the robber chief growled.

Debu swallowed. Perhaps the truth might be his best support, as it had been with the Lama. Haltingly, he repeated his story.

'No father!' The chief's wide nostrils flared with fury. He eyed him shrewdly. 'You're trying to put us off!'

'Why would I do that?' Debu's voice choked. 'Won't it be worse for me?'

The chief glowered at him as if trying to make up his mind to believe him or not. 'A real beggar we've picked up!' he snarled.

'I told you to finish him off, Nangbo.'

'Kill me if you wish!' Debu cried. 'But remember, the Lama has taken me under his special protection. His men must have told him already. If they find you killed me, when they catch you, your punishment will be really severe.'

'Quiet!' the chief thundered. 'You dare say such things to me?'

But for all his bravado, Debu noticed that he looked uncertain. That meant what Jeevan had told him was true—that robbers were brutally chastised if they were caught, even whipped to death. Absently Nangbo put the cup of chhang to his mouth again. Once he had taken another long draught, he growled, 'I don't kill children . . .' Then he frowned. 'Well, boy, since you're no good for ransom, you'll have to work for your keep . . . till we decide what to do with you.'

Debu heaved a sigh of relief. In the meantime the Lama might ask the officials to send some men to search for him. Kalyan Singh might discover what had happened and appeal to the Jongpen.

But as the days passed and nothing happened, Debu struggled to keep his hopes alive. The robbers kept him on the run. He brewed their tea, boiled their soup and filled their cups with chhang. Fortunately they were not a large gang. In fact, they seemed to be quite hard up. Recalling the stories that he had heard, of robber bands rich and powerful enough to threaten officials, he was thankful. From the snatches of conversation he overheard, he learned that they'd been through a spell of bad luck lately. Their loot had been limited and their victims had often been able to fight them off. They had also lost several members of their gang.

Debu discovered too, that the chief had spared him because he was afraid to invite further misfortune by killing a boy favoured by the Lama.

When he finally realized no one would come to save him, Debu's despair intensified. He fought it by plotting his escape. He began to watch the robbers' movements closely and eavesdrop on their future plans.

The bandits did not follow any specific routine. They prepared for their raids by making ammunition, using saltpetre, which they extracted from the manure of sheep and goats by burning it. The bullets were cut out of yaks' horns because of the shortage of lead, which was often used just to weight them.

One evening the band saddled up and left on what seemed to be an unplanned foray. Debu was left behind with two old men.

The robbers returned two days later. The sun had already gone down and Debu was lighting a fire to stew the evening soup when the first riders trotted into the camp dispiritedly—Dingmo and Chumbel.

'Hold my horse, boy!' Dingmo rapped out. Puppet-like, Debu moved to obey. As Dingmo alighted and Debu took the horse's reins, the robber kicked him unexpectedly hard on the shin.

'That's for not moving fast enough,' he said. Debu gulped hard. Limping, he led the horse away. As he unsaddled it and filled its feeding trough, he was startled to feel a sympathetic hand warm on his shoulder. It was Chumbel.

'Never mind, Debu,' he said. 'He's in a foul mood—we—we didn't get anything.'

Debu squashed his face against the horse's neck. He didn't want Chumbel to see how moved he was. To his surprise, the horse whinnied softly. A silver-grey pony, it had always reminded him of Bijli. A strange thought sprang to his mind . . .

When the band had retired for the night, and Debu lay sleepless in his bed, he heard a footstep. The sharp odour of turmeric pricked his nostrils. 'Here, this will soothe the pain.' It was Chumbel again. He put a warm rag smeared with turmeric and rock salt on his aching leg and bound it with a piece of string, then left silently.

The treatment worked because the pain vanished by the next morning. However, when he went up to thank him, Chumbel hurriedly moved away. But Debu was grateful to have one friend at least.

That night, a desperate thought surfaced. Debu sat up, listening to the sounds of the night, a robber's guttural snores, the muzzy bleat of a sheep in the distance and the harsh sighing of the wind. Quiet as a mouse he crept out, then crawled to the horses' tent, just in case someone glimpsed his silhouette.

The odour of animal dung was strong in his nostrils. Heart racing, his eyes sought the grey horse in the hazy dark. The steed did not resist when he saddled it, because Debu whispered softly in its ear, the way he talked to Bijli. Silent as a ghost, he led it out and mounted it only when he was outside the camp. As he warmed to a gallop, it took all his will power to resist the temptation to speed away, following the road as far as it went.

It's just a trial run, he reminded himself, to see if I can take a ride undetected. To escape I'll have to be better prepared. But this stolen ride was so exhilarating that Debu felt as buoyant as a cloud when he led the horse back and sneaked into bed again. Thankfully no one had noticed. He couldn't help repeating his midnight foray once more, despite the risk. This time too he got away, which made him think of a serious plan.

Then another dark night came, much like the one on which they had captured him. The robbers had been preparing for another raid. There was the usual activity, the same feeling of anticipation. Debu guessed this was something major—much talk had preceded it.

The evening meal was eaten earlier than usual. Then the horses were saddled, the guns loaded. Unlike the other two occasions, the robbers seemed morose, even anxious. Debu could guess why. Their stock of food was running low; they had even slaughtered a couple of sheep a few days ago, something they avoided,

Chumbel told him. They preferred to sell them and distribute the spoils.

If only they'd take me along, Debu thought suddenly as he watched them get ready to leave. At least I'd get out of the camp. But he didn't dare ask.

He watched them mounting their horses, wondering if he should pray they had luck, if that would make his life easier. Suddenly Nangbo wheeled around and grabbed his throat. A scream rose to Debu's lips. But to his astonishment, Nangbo simply barked, 'Give me that charm!'

Debu pulled it off with trembling hands and handed it to him. Then he turned away, with the robber chief's yell 'Ullu-llu-llu!' resounding in his ears. The others took up the cry and the horde galloped off, their silhouettes eerie in the smoky-grey light.

As Debu crawled under the stinking blankets, he almost prayed that they would be successful. He could claim that he had brought them good fortune and ask Nangbo to let him join them next time.

The sound of triumphant yells jerked Debu awake the next morning. He rushed out of his tent to be deafened by the baaing of frightened sheep and the high-pitched whinnies of protesting horses. A broad grin split Chumbel's face as he drove several sheep and goats into the camp, herding them expertly into the enclosure. 'Your charm proved lucky,' he whispered in Debu's ear. 'Nangbo's delighted.'

And as Debu watched, Nangbo screamed 'Ullu-llu-llu!' as he galloped around the camp.

The rest took up the cry. Finding the robber chief's eye on him, Debu joined in, impulsively. Nangbo hooted with laughter. He jumped off his horse and tapped Debu's back lightly with his whip. Then he groped at his waist, opened his moneybag, took out a few coins and flung them at Debu, saying, 'Catch!'

Startled, Debu couldn't react fast enough, and the coins scattered on the ground. Nangbo nodded and gestured towards them. Debu smarted at the humiliation, then something told him this was not the moment to be proud. So he bent and gathered up the coins. Silver tankas! Eight of them! Guiltily he wondered to whom they had belonged, but remembered to fold his hands in thanks.

The following day two of the bandits went to dispose of the goods in the nearest market town. The rest of the gang spent their time riding around the camp and practising tricks, preparing ammunition or just sleeping.

But Nangbo was already planning his next venture, Chumbel told him. Now that his luck had turned, he wished to make up his losses as fast as he could. And this raid would be a far more ambitious one.

PREPARING FOR A RAID

'We should get ready to raid Thok Jalong now,' Debu heard Nangbo say one evening, as he brought him his hookah.

'Too far,' Dingmo objected. 'And there aren't enough of us. You know the miners are always well armed.'

'It's worth the risk,' the chief insisted. 'A few large nuggets of gold will go a long way. And then,' he smiled, fingering the amulet at his neck, 'our luck has changed. It's time to strike it rich.'

The short man remained sullenly silent. 'You're satisfied with what we're doing right now?' Nangbo's face darkened. 'Just hunting for two or three stray travellers, grabbing a couple of yaks and a few sacks of barley flour? Unless we take chances we'll never lay our hands on any decent booty.' His gaze swept the faces of the men gathered there. 'What do you all say?'

Most of them nodded emphatically. 'Let Dingmo stay back if he's afraid,' a robber named Dorjya sniggered. 'We're ready. Who doesn't want to put away a few nuggets for his old age?'

Debu's heart, which had leapt momentarily, sank again. He had decided to ask Nangbo to take him along and was hoping that they'd plan a raid somewhere nearer Gartok. It would give him a chance to get away. He knew all about Thok Jalong, the fabled gold mines. The traders brought back gold or gold dust, which came from the mines. His mother had owned earrings, a choker and bracelets made from Tibetan gold.

Later, when he probed Chumbel for details, he learned that Thok Jalong was several days' march from the camp. Debu decided it would be better to stay back. The robbers would be away for a long time, providing him with the perfect opportunity to escape. It would be easy to hoodwink the two old men. All he needed was a horse. And . . . though Dingmo would take his silver-grey pony, there was an old horse they usually left behind. Debu's heart quickened. It didn't matter if the horse was slow. He could cover enough distance in a night to make it difficult for the two old men to catch up. He would use the stars to keep track of the direction and follow the laptches that marked the road. Sooner or later he would arrive at a village, a monastery, or if he got really lucky, a trading centre.

But the morning before the raid, as he was leaving Nangbo's tent after serving tea, the robber said, 'Listen, boy.'

93

'Yes, master.' Debu had learned to use the falsely humble tone that kept the robber chief in good humour.

'You will come with us tonight!'

'Co—come with you?'

'Yes! You are sturdy enough and I've noticed that you can ride well.'

Debu's mouth went dry. Had Nangbo been watching him? To his relief he didn't look annoyed, amused rather, even approving. What a strange fellow he was, sometimes unbelievably savage, almost kindly at others! Debu knew, however, that Nangbo might appear whimsical but was coldly calculating too. That's how he managed to keep the rebellious Dingmo in his place.

Then Dingmo snapped, 'Wait a minute! First you want to attempt a task as impossible as raiding Thok Jalong, then you want to take this child along!'

'Child? He's as tall as you and as strong possibly. I've seen him handling the yaks. And I'm sure he knows how to handle a gun. Don't you, boy?'

Debu hesitated. He wasn't sure whether he should admit that his father had taught him to shoot two years back.

Nangbo took his silence for assent and said, 'He can shoot.'

Dingmo face darkened. 'So have you seen him shoot too?' he said. 'Since when have our prisoners been allowed to use our guns?'

'You . . .!' Nangbo whirled to his feet. 'I'll show you that the boy can shoot. I don't have to see. I can look into a person's mind! You all know that!'

Dingmo paled as Nangbo's lip curled menacingly.

The chief's gaze swept over the assembled gang and his voice was chillingly low as he said, 'You know that, don't you?'

The rest of the robbers nodded as though hypnotized. Nangbo stared at them for a while then his mood changed again. He smiled, saying briskly, 'Come along!' He picked up one of the guns hanging from a hook and strode out of the tent.

Debu had no choice but to follow, though his mouth was as dry as paper and his heart thumped like an out-of-beat drum. If he let the chief down, all the goodwill he had gained recently would vanish. But . . . if he displayed his skill in shooting, he would have to go on the raid . . .

His hands shook as he took the rifle into his hand. It was similar to the one his father had. Nangbo pointed to a post in the yard. 'Come on! Hit that!'

But as Debu put the gun to his shoulder and took sight, his confusion vanished. He'd try his best to hit the post; he had to stay on the right side of Nangbo.

Then another thought made his pulse race. Suppose . . . he turned the gun around and aimed it at Nangbo . . . kept the robbers at bay . . . grabbed a horse . . . escaped? Then doubt entered his mind again. They'd be upon him in a trice. But suppose he never got an opportunity again?

He could feel the silence around him. 'Come on, boy!' Nangbo cried out. Debu's finger pressed the trigger almost automatically. He felt the recoil hard on his shoulder, followed by the blast, which deafened him. He blinked, shook his head. Should he try?

95

But suddenly . . . his whole body seemed to freeze. He could not move . . . or even open his mouth. He could see Nangbo's eyes fixed on him, mockingly. Then the chief took the gun from his hands and his paralysis disappeared as mysteriously as it had come.

'See! He's an excellent shot! He shot off the top of the post!' Nangbo smirked at the sullen Dingmo.

Chumbel was thumping him on his back, the other robbers clapping and cheering. Dingmo's mouth twisted with disgust and he spat noisily. Debu looked up at Nangbo, numb with fear. Could he have read his mind? It was a chilling thought. Debu stumbled away, head bowed, not even feeling the congratulatory pats on his back.

'You don't look too happy,' Chumbel told him as they fed the horses later in the afternoon.

When Debu remained silent, he said, 'I know you're longing to go back to your people.' His eyes were soft with sympathy. 'But for your own good, let me tell you'll never be able to escape. First, you don't know the way. You'd get lost and die of hunger and thirst. And then . . .' His face turned grim. 'Nangbo can be extremely vengeful if he's crossed . . . Right now he feels you're lucky for the gang. He'll keep you here at all costs.'

'Help me, Chumbel,' Debu pleaded, gripping his hand, as despair overwhelmed him. 'Please help me get away!'

Chumbel stared at him aghast, then jerked his arm away, looking around fearfully. 'Don't even dream of it! You don't know Nangbo. He has eyes at the back of his head . . . ears that can pick up sounds miles away.' He lowered his voice. 'Some say he has captured a spirit who guides him.'

Debu swallowed the hysterical laughter that rose to his throat. Chumbel's response was such a shock. 'If he has, why is he having such bad luck?' he asked bitterly.

'Because of Dingmo's plots. They say he has found an equally powerful spirit and is trying to take control of the gang. But,' his voice went lower still, 'since he took your amulet, Nangbo has found protection against Dingmo's magic.'

Debu didn't know what to say. Like others in his village he too believed in talismans and magic words, also in spirits that took possession of people. But not to the extent Chumbel and his comrades did.

'If you're taken into the gang and have the chief's favour, it'll be good for you.' Chumbel tried to console him. 'And we're going to make much in this raid. You'll get your share. Nangbo's absolutely fair. Didn't he give you the coins the other day?'

Debu sighed, nodded and said shortly, 'Perhaps you're right.'

It was obvious that he had no choice. He would just have to bide his time. But how long? He might be trapped here for months. In the meantime his fellow traders would go back. What would his mother feel when she was told that like his father, he too had got lost in Tibet? The thought was just too horrible to contemplate, as was that of being stuck here forever, part of a robber band.

TO THE GOLDFIELDS

The preparations were over, provisions for the journey loaded, the horses saddled.

'You will ride beside me, boy,' Nangbo's eyes narrowed. 'Remember, no tricks! And you, Chumbel, you will watch him from the other side.'

Chumbel's face shrank with terror. 'Yes, yes, my master,' he said. 'Just as you say!' He threw a warning glance at Debu.

Debu forced himself to sound enthusiastic and say, 'Do you think I'd be so foolish, my chief? I'm as eager as anyone else to pick up some gold nuggets.'

Nangbo smiled crookedly, but his eyes still searched Debu's face.

The robbers' war cry rang out and they were on the road, the hoof beats of the horses matching the drumming of Debu's heart. Because despite everything, a rush of excitement overcame him and the smile that wreathed his face as Nangbo turned to glance at him was genuine. The robber's face seemed to soften and relax as he looked away and rode along at a steady pace.

It was the first time Debu was leaving the camp since that fateful night. How many days was it? He had tried to keep track in the beginning, by making notches on a wooden post. But somewhere along he had missed out one day, then another, and given up. At best he could guess it might be three to four weeks.

Dawn had not broken but the sky was lightening into a luminous lemon-grey. A rather dented looking moon was still visible, as were a few fading stars. If I manage to get away from all this, Debu thought, what stories I will have to tell.

The day was far advanced when he saw something moving on the lonely road, far ahead. As they came closer, he realized it was a caravan.

'A caravan!' Chumbel echoed his thoughts, throwing a significant glance at the chief. Debu's pulse raced. Were the robbers thinking of attacking it? Or could he appeal to them for help, or . . .?

Nangbo shook his head. Debu could guess why. The caravan was too large, and gigantic guards accompanied it, well armed with rifles and spears. It was an impressive sight though—the sun's rays caught the brilliant gold-and-blue brocade robes the men wore, their green silk hats, and the ornate silver scabbards hanging at their waists. The women were as lavishly dressed, sported elaborate headdresses and velvet boots. As they came close, Debu gazed at their faces, astonished. They were wearing painted yak skin masks.

'It's to protect their complexions from the sun,' Chumbel murmured. He dismounted and bowed, sticking out his tongue, as did some of the others. It was a display of respect to someone socially superior and a clever ploy. Debu noticed the distrustful glances the others flung at them. Nangbo bowed too, without getting off his horse.

With a pang Debu heard the caravan recede, not daring to turn around for a last glimpse. Nangbo was watching.

In the evening they set up camp on the wayside. The horses were hobbled with iron-hinged fetters and tents set up on either side, flanking them. Debu helped Chumbel to light a fire while some of the other robbers hunted for dried animal dung for fuel. There seemed to be a good supply because many herds passed this way.

Once the fire was lit, he put the usual dinner on to cook—a soup of boiled meat, which Chumbel thickened with a few pinches of flour and dried buttermilk powder. The meal over, they retreated to bed.

'The boy will sleep in my tent,' Nangbo said. Debu quietly went and brought his blankets.

He was about to crawl into bed, when Nangbo, who was nursing a cup of chhang, suddenly said, 'Do you know I was as old as you when I went out on my first raid?'

'Oh, is that so?' Debu replied politely. He was tired and longed to sleep. But Nangbo was in a mood to talk. Debu wondered how old he could be. It was hard to make out from his weather-beaten face. But he moved like a man who couldn't be more than thirty.

'I am a Khampa,' Nangbo continued. 'My father was a rich man with large herds.'

Debu sat up, his curiosity spurting.

'So, how . . . did you take up this work?' he asked carefully.

'My older brother was a terrible bully. He always beat me. When my father fell ill and died, he wouldn't give me my share. Finding an opportunity, one day I stole some horses and ran away. By chance the caravan I was travelling with was attacked. I told the robbers I would join them if they spared me. The chief favoured me and I took his place when he died of his wounds after a raid . . .'

'Do you like this life?' Debu couldn't resist asking.

Nangbo's eyes glittered. 'I am feared,' he said. 'Once I spared a lama's life when I was raiding a party. He could tell the future and said I would be very rich.'

He examined Debu's face and said, 'He also gave me a mantra which would give me power over men.'

Debu felt a twinge of fear. Why was he telling him all this? 'They—they say you have a spirit under your control.'

Nangbo threw back his head and laughed heartily. 'Do they? Do—do you want to see him?'

'No,' Debu said, gulping. 'No . . .'

'Don't be afraid,' Nangbo said softly. 'I won't allow it to harm you.'

But Debu's breath had stopped, because Nangbo's

eyes had become fixed and glassy, his body seemed to quiver, and his breath came loud and quick. He began to speak in a loud guttural voice. And as Debu watched . . . his body seemed to lift off the ground and float!

Debu's palms turned clammy despite the cold, his breath bottled up inside his throat, suffocating him. His terror mounted to an unbearable pitch.

Then unexpectedly Nangbo slipped back on to the ground and rolled over as if in a faint. Debu started up and ran to him. He knelt over him, wondering what he should do, when all of a sudden, the chief opened his eyes.

'Ah, it's you, boy. Go to bed. We have a long march tomorrow.' He rose as if nothing unusual had happened and flinging off his coat, lay down and pulled his fur blanket over him.

Debu lay awake for a while, trembling till Nangbo's snores told him he was sound asleep. Then, overcome by sheer exhaustion, he dozed off too.

When they set off early next morning, he wondered if it had actually happened or he had imagined it. But the robber chief was taciturn and thoughtful and spoke little to anyone when they broke for tea at around ten o'clock as they usually did.

Debu could glimpse snow-capped mountains in the distance, and they passed a couple of lakes. But Chumbel told him the water was brackish and they refilled their leather water bags from a stream.

'How long is it now before we reach Thok Jalong?'

he asked Chumbel when they began to set up camp again.

'Another day perhaps,' was his reply.

The landscape was as grim as Debu's mood as they made their way towards the goldfields. Grey clouds stretched over the sky and the wind was like a brutal knife. They toiled over a pass and rode on towards a desolate plain. Thok Jalong stood at an altitude of 16,000 feet, he had heard. When the settlement of black yak hair tents came into view, a surge of curiosity wiped out his dejection.

They set up camp well out of sight that afternoon. After an early supper, Nangbo summoned the group. 'We will attack tonight,' he said. 'Remember, everything hinges on the swiftness of our assault. Throw them into confusion and grab whatever you can.' His gaze whirled over the silent band and his thick brows drew together.

Then Nangbo closed his eyes and seemed to be muttering something under his breath. The rest of the group watched, rigid. As for Dingmo, his bravado seemed to have deserted him. He'd been glum and silent throughout the journey.

At last Nangbo opened his eyes and took a deep breath. 'This place smells of good fortune, my spirit tells me!' He smiled and the robbers broke into subdued cheers.

Debu's heart thudded painfully as they tiptoed towards the horses. It was a dark night and the moon was yet to rise. This could be my chance, he thought, a fragile hope springing up again. Maybe I can slip away, warn the miners!

It vanished when Nangbo said, 'Wait a minute, boy. You will share Chumbel's horse.'

'Are you mad?' Dingmo said angrily. 'It'll slow the horse down if it has to carry two people.'

'And if the boy runs away? Tries to warn the miners?' Debu's blood turned to ice.

Reluctantly he mounted Chumbel's horse and sat behind him. Worse, they tied him securely to the saddle. However, a rifle was handed to him.

'If you show yourself to be as good a shot as you were in the camp, next time you can go in on your own,' Nangbo said, with a mocking smile.

Debu shivered. Nangbo expected him to kill, or at least wound someone! How could he?

'He brought you for luck,' Chumbel whispered. 'The spirit must have told him to do so. And he's giving you a chance.'

Debu didn't answer.

'Move!' Nangbo commanded.

The band made its way down the slope, silent as shadows. Stealthily, the robbers approached a cluster of tents somewhat away from the rest. Two men dismounted and crept towards them to cut the ropes. They were just a few feet way when a dog's loud bark rang out, then another and another!

'Quick!' shouted the chief. 'Grab some horses.' As the night came alive with the deep, hoarse barks of the Tibetan mastiffs, he wheeled towards a large tent.

The restless tramp of horses' hooves and sounds of neighing came from it.

Debu could hear people shouting as they came awake. Shots rang out from the tents. The robbers fired back. As Debu jogged along uncomfortably, he heard the normally even-tempered Chumbel curse. A twinge of fear needled him. Everyone was firing at random. Some of the tent ropes had been cut and he could see people struggling beneath them.

Dingmo and one or two other robbers unfettered some horses and were already galloping up the slope. Debu fired as their horse carried them towards the shadowy figures emerging from the tents, keeping the gun pointed to the ground so no one would be hurt. A man fell down and Nangbo's war cry rang out behind him. The chief was holding a short sword and striking out expertly at the dark figures multiplying before them. Shouts and yells merged with the pounding of hooves and the animals' cries as the robber chief swept through the group like a whirlwind bringing havoc.

Zing! Something whistled past Debu's ear. Mechanically he ducked. But Chumbel shrieked. Debu felt a tremendous jerk, as if someone had pushed him from behind. And found he was flying off the horse, along with Chumbel!

Thud! He hit the ground with a force that jolted each and every bone in his body. The last thing he heard was an agonizing cry of pain . . .

SAVED!

When Debu came to in the faint grey light, for a few moments he thought he was back home. His brain felt fuzzy, as if he'd woken up from a deep sleep. As his eyes got used to the dimness, he realized that he was lying in a tent. Where was he—with the caravan from his village? Then slowly the events of the last few days unfurled in his mind and he felt a sickening lurch of dismay. He was still with the robbers and injured to boot. How badly was he hurt? Gingerly, he touched his head. There was a cloth tied around it—it felt soft and smooth, like fine cotton. Debu's confusion grew. The robbers wouldn't bandage his head with such material, would they? His hands fell back, too weak to hold themselves up any longer.

Debu's ears searched for the familiar sounds of the robber camp, a voice raised in command, argument or laughter, the neighing of a horse. But he heard nothing. Then, as he turned on his side and tried to raise himself up, he felt a woolly animal skin beneath him. And just as he was throwing off the rough blanket that covered him, he heard a soft step and a woman's voice: the first he'd heard in a long, long time. 'Oh, so you're awake?'

Debu found himself looking at a round, red-cheeked, smiling face.

'Yes,' he managed to croak.

'It's all right. Don't talk too much, you're badly hurt, running a temperature too. Here, drink this. It'll keep the fever down.' She lifted his head and put a bowl to his lips. It was a strange brew, neither bitter nor sweet. Debu gulped it down and sank back again, still puzzled but grateful. He wanted to ask her who she was and where he was, but his eyelids were becoming heavy again and the words died on his lips.

When Debu awoke the next time, his head ached less and his mind felt clearer. He sat up, taking in his surroundings: the black woollen walls of the tent, the old rugs covering the ground, a rather weather-beaten chest in a corner with a wooden cup placed on it. It did not look very different from the robbers' tent, but *felt* different. It was almost as if he were back home with his mother fussing over him.

The light was so weak that it was hard to make out the time. So he sat up and tried to get to his feet. To his dismay his legs buckled under him.

'Careful!' The woman ran and helped him back

into the bed. 'It'll take you some time to recover your strength,' she said.

Debu waited for the dizziness to subside, then asked. 'Where am I?'

The woman examined him for a moment before replying.

She had a cheerful face with her hair plaited into numerous braids, and wore necklaces of large coral and gold beads. She could have been his mother's age, Debu thought. 'At Thok Jalong, the goldfields,' she replied, still watching him warily.

Debu smiled faintly. So . . . I got left behind, he thought. The miners must believe him to be a robber. Yet they had taken care of him.

'How long have I been like this?' he asked. 'What happened to me?'

'Three days,' the woman replied, her tone neutral. 'We found you lying unconscious on the ground.'

'I—I am not really one of the robbers,' he said quickly. He had to try and clear himself. Would she believe him, though?

'What were you doing with the robbers, then?' she asked. 'We were surprised to find you tied to the one who got killed. Why did they do that? Several of our people were injured too,' she added.

'He was killed?' Debu gasped. 'Oh! Poor Chumbel. I had a lucky escape.' He was silent for a while, mourning his friend. 'What happened to the others?'

'They got away,' the woman frowned. 'They took some of our best horses too,' she added indignantly.

'Did they manage to get any gold?'

'No,' she said, her frown deepening. 'We know how to protect ourselves.'

'I'm happy to hear that,' he said, brightening. Then it hit him. He had escaped! He might have got hurt, but he could get on with his quest now.

The woman's voice broke into his thoughts. 'So, you're not really one of them?' she asked.

'Of course not!' Debu cried out. 'You can't believe how happy I am to have escaped. I'd been plotting and planning, searching for such an opportunity for days. I still can't believe that it's actually happened!'

'We were a little confused since you were so young. Why did they bring you along, then?' she asked.

Then he told her his story, how he had come searching for his father, been detained by the Lama and fallen prey to the robbers. Also how Nangbo had wanted to initiate him into the gang.

'So that was why you were tied to the other man. Ah, poor child,' she said. 'I thought there was something different about you. Even the way you speak our language. But I thought you might be from another part of the country.'

She told him that her name was Dolma and her husband a miner working in the goldfields.

'You can stay with us as long as you wish,' Dolma smiled. 'We'd be really happy to keep you . . . We don't have any children of our own . . . And now, let me get you something to eat.'

Debu was touched. He could make out that though

110

they were mining for gold, they were not very well off. The thought that she had nursed him so devotedly, even though she suspected him to be a robber, made his eyes overflow. But there was only one thought in his mind.

'How can I get to Gartok?' he asked eagerly, when she came back with a bowl of hot soup. 'The other people from my village were headed there . . . and I was hoping to find out something about my father too.'

'Wait till you're better,' she said. 'Caravans leave regularly from here, and you can join one as soon as you're fit to travel.'

When he finished, Dolma rose, took his bowl away, and then Debu heard her say, 'Ah, you're back. The sick boy's better.' She lowered her voice and though Debu strained to overhear, he couldn't make anything out. He could only see a small, bent figure, silhouetted in the dim light. Dolma's husband had come back from work. Would he be as sympathetic as she was? Stoically he prepared himself for the worst.

But his fears turned out to be ill-founded. 'So you are a Shauka? I'm Tsering.' A skinny man with twinkling black eyes stood there. He gazed at Debu and murmured, 'From the land of the blessed Buddha himself.' He continued, 'I have met some traders from India in Gartok. But never a boy as young as you.'

'I'm looking for my father,' Debu said simply.

'So Dolma says. May the gracious Lord Buddha help you,' the man folded his hands reverently. 'You

111

know, this wife of mine insisted on nursing you, though some people felt you should be left to die.'

'I am extremely grateful to her,' Debu said. 'May Lord Buddha shower his blessings on both of you too,' he added.

Both husband and wife bowed their heads.

THE MINERS

Debu couldn't bear to wait to find out about the next caravan to Gartok, though it took two whole days before his legs felt strong enough to support him. The traders usually stayed in Tibet for two to three months. After that it was risky because the weather changed and the passes got blocked with snow. He had been at Nangbo's camp for almost a month and couldn't afford to lose any more time.

On the third morning, after breakfast Debu asked Dolma, 'Can I go and take a look at the goldfields, maybe find out about the caravan?'

She looked at him doubtfully. 'Do you think you are strong enough?'

'Of course,' he said. 'You've been feeding me so well.'

'As you wish,' she said. 'I'll come with you, just in case.'

That might not be a bad idea, Debu thought. She could help him to find out about the caravans. He climbed out of the strange dwelling—a sort of pit dug in the ground with a tent pitched on it. His legs were a little rubbery still and the sunlight made him blink, after all those days inside the dark tent.

The icy wind hit him with such force that he had to dig his legs in to brace himself against it. So that's why the miners lived underground! The wind would probably freeze them to death while they slept, if they didn't. But it did help in one way. It seemed to clear his head.

He walked on unsteadily, following Dolma out of the wilderness of tents. It would have been hard to find his way back if he'd been alone.

'There they are,' Dolma said.

Debu gazed at the long, deep trench that stretched on and on. To think that all this reddish-brown soil was full of gold!

'Can anyone work the mines?' he asked.

'You have to pay taxes,' Dolma told him, 'to the official in charge, the Sarpen.' She sighed. 'The truth is you can earn more by keeping sheep and goats or trading. There's much less gold than there used to be.'

'Is that so?' Debu asked, surprised. 'I thought digging for gold would be the quickest way to get rich. I've heard tales about the huge nuggets found here.'

'It doesn't happen too often.' Dolma shook her head.

The miners were at work, singing in chorus. They were scooping up soil in baskets, placing it on cloth sieves, then washing it with water from the stream that ran through the bottom of the trench. The mud got sluiced away and the gold was left behind. For a while Debu stood there watching them.

Dolma said, 'It's hard work, but we do keep hoping too that one day Tsering will find a big lump of gold.' Her broad cheeks crinkled. 'Perhaps we can return to our village near Lhasa then and settle down to farming.'

Debu thought of Nangbo coming here with the same hope—to find gold. How long ago it seemed now! 'Where's your husband working?' he asked.

Dolma shaded her eyes to peer into the distance. 'I can't see him,' she said. 'The mine stretches for about a mile. He works further away. It'll be too tiring for you to go there.'

Debu nodded. He wanted to ask where he could find out about the caravan but hesitated. Would it look rude if he kept harping on it? She'd been so kind to him.

Then, as he turned away to look around him, he saw something moving in the distance. A long line of yaks laden with goods, ponies and men—a caravan!

Debu's heart jerked. The caravan was leaving! Who knew when the next one would go? He had to join it, somehow! He tried to leap over the pit, ignoring Dolma's agitated shouts.

An uneven mound of earth caught his toe, and he fell straight into the trench, all the breath knocked out of him. He lay there—the smell of earth thick in his nostrils, trying to gather the strength to get up again.

115

A strong arm hoisted him up and dusted him down roughly. 'Eh! Where do you think you're going? You nearly buried Chancho!'

Debu stared into a miner's sun-scorched face. He looked around for Chancho but couldn't see him. 'I—I'm sorry,' Debu said. 'I didn't see where I was going.'

'That you should be,' the man growled. He picked up his broad brimmed hat, shook off the mud and spat loudly.

'*Thoo*! Chancho's mouth is full of dust. Even if it's got gold in it, it doesn't taste good! Henh, boy? Do you think gold dust tastes good?'

Debu smiled. The miner himself was Chancho! To his relief, Chancho's eyes were twinkling, so he said, 'I'm sure it doesn't, sir.'

The man grinned, showing broken yellow teeth, then looked hard at Debu. 'You're the Shauka boy, aren't you? From India? The one who was with the robbers?'

Debu nodded. 'Yes . . .' Then he went on, feeling an explanation was necessary. 'I—I saw the caravan leaving and wanted to catch up with it. In case it was leaving for Gartok.'

'You want to go to Gartok? Hmmm . . . that's where you people trade . . .' He gazed at Debu, tugging at the few hairs straggling on his chin. 'How did you land up with the robbers?'

Then Debu heard shrill cries and looked up to see Dolma standing at the edge, wringing her hands. 'I'm all right,' he yelled. 'I'm just coming out! It's the lady who took care of me,' he smiled at the miner.

But the man's questioning gaze was still fixed on him so he told him about his quest, briefly.

Chancho closed one eye. He seemed to be thinking so hard that Debu was afraid he might pull out his whole beard! 'Looking for your father, eh? Well . . . it's quite a coincidence, but there are one or two Shaukas here. It's a rare thing—they may know something, though we're pretty far from Gartok.'

'Will you ask them please?' Debu asked eagerly. 'I'll be back tomorrow.'

'All right. Chancho will help you, even though you made him eat dust,' the man thumped him playfully on his back.

'Thank you, Uncle Chancho,' Debu said, smiling.

He glanced up again to see Dolma standing there, a puzzled look on her face. She beckoned to him impatiently. The caravan must be out of sight by now, and he was cold and badly shaken. He drew his coat more closely about him, tucked in his chin, said goodbye to Chancho and climbed out.

'Whatever possessed you to run off like that?' Dolma asked, annoyed.

'I—I saw the caravan leaving at a distance,' Debu said miserably. 'I thought if I ran fast enough I might be able to catch it.'

Dolma didn't scold him for his foolishness, just drew him close and said, 'Poor child, you're really eager to go and start looking for your father again, aren't you?' Debu nodded, then said eagerly, 'The miner I fell on top of, Chancho, told me there are one or two Shaukas working here in the mine.'

117

'Is that so?' Dolma's brow furrowed. 'I've never heard of any before. I'll ask my husband to find out. And,' she continued, 'I'll ask him to find out too, when the next caravan is leaving for Gartok and see if you can join it.'

'Oh! How can I thank you!' Debu hugged Dolma.

Dolma beamed and hugged him back. 'You can thank me by listening to me because now you need to go home and rest.'

'I think so too,' Debu replied. The excitement had been too much. His legs felt shaky again and the dizziness seemed to overtake him. It was an effort to make the trek back to the camp.

A bowl of hot soup revived him somewhat, but Dolma insisted he rest, though he offered to help her with her household chores. He was getting fed up of lying down and doing nothing the whole day.

When Tsering came in the evening and heard about the day's events, he said, 'It is possible that there are Shaukas working the mines.' The fine lines on his face deepened as he smiled. 'Don't worry, child, I'll ask around. I will also inquire about the caravan.' His face grew a little serious and he turned away and picked up his prayer wheel and began to whirl it silently. Tsering was extremely religious. In fact, Dolma had jokingly said yesterday, 'He really should have joined a monastery.'

As Debu watched the colourful, beaded ribbons that hung from the prayer wheel spinning, waves of regret washed over him.

He had grown fond of the kind couple. And he knew that Tsering, though not as demonstrative as Dolma, had become deeply attached to him. But he had to find his father. To make it up to Dolma, he spent the next day at home, pottering around doing little jobs. He couldn't risk going out into the cold wind and falling ill again.

But a couple of days passed and Tsering was unable to find anything definite. Debu thought it was time he became more active.

'I ought to go around asking, Uncle,' he said. 'I'm feeling much better now.'

Dolma's brow furrowed. 'Are you sure?' she asked.

'Of course, Auntie,' Debu insisted. 'I wouldn't think of it if I wasn't. I don't want to fall ill again.'

Tsering looked at him doubtfully. Then he sighed and said, 'Maybe you'll be able to learn more. It's possible that the men are afraid to let others know. I'm not sure if they are permitted to work here.'

Dolma bundled Debu up warmly in a sheepskin coat and he set off. He decided to go to the western edge of the goldfields. He would cover the whole dig systematically, however long it took. And if he found Chancho again, he could ask him too if he had learned anything.

But the first day was full of disappointment. The miner he approached first, a tall fellow with unkempt hair falling from beneath his wide-brimmed hat, glared at him suspiciously, saying, 'Why should a Shauka be here?' Then he brought his broad face close to Debu's

119

and hissed, 'If you find one, you better tell me. I'll show the fellow where he ought to be!'

Debu stumbled away, alarmed. The encounter discouraged him so much that he wondered whether he ought to go back and just wait for the next caravan to Gartok. Even if one or two Shaukas were working here, there was a slim chance that they'd know anything about his father. He climbed out of the dig and made his way back to the tent.

Dolma sensed his disappointment right away. 'Don't get disheartened,' she said. 'Sooner or later I'm sure you'll get some news.'

Tsering, who was already back, echoed her words. 'There are a few people leaving for Gartok in a couple of days,' he said. 'I have spoken to the leader—they'll take you along. But there's one thing . . .' he paused, biting his lip.

'Do I have to pay something?' Debu asked.

'Don't worry about that,' Tsering said quickly. 'Actually you'll need a horse or jibbo to travel.'

A horse or jibbo! Debu had been so preoccupied that these practical problems had not crossed his mind at all.

But how could he get hold of a horse? Then a thought flashed through his mind. The tankas! The ones Nangbo had given him! Would they be enough? Not likely . . . but there was something else . . . the gold coin he had concealed in the sole of his boots when he set out on his journey. He'd completely forgotten about it.

'Uncle!' he cried. 'I have some money.' He pulled out the little cloth pouch in which he had kept the coins.

'The robber chief gave these to me one day when he was in a good mood . . . and . . . I have a gold coin too. I hid it in my boot. Luckily the robbers didn't find it when they captured me!'

'Oh, child!' Tsering shook his head. 'You didn't need to worry about the money. We would have managed it.'

'No, no! You've done more than enough!' Debu cried. 'I can never thank you sufficiently.'

'You don't need to, child,' Dolma hugged him. 'We were only too happy to have you here.'

She forced extra soup on him that night. 'You need to keep your strength up,' she smiled. 'You should rest tomorrow. The journey will be hard. There's no point tramping about in the cold all day.'

A MYSTERY REVEALED

But Debu felt too restless to follow her advice. Early next morning, after Tsering left, he trudged to the northern limits of the camp. A group of miners were already at work. Debu thought he'd just walk on the surface looking around. If luck favoured him, he might come across one of the Shauka miners.

But it was hard to get a proper look at the men's faces. For a while he rambled along, wondering if it was any use continuing the search. Then a group of them stopped singing to discuss something. Their animated voices aroused Debu's curiosity. He went down on his haunches to peer into the pit. Could someone have found a good-sized nugget?

One of the men glanced up and fixed a curious gaze on him. Debu called out hesitantly, 'Friend, do you know of any Shaukas working here?'

'I can't hear you!' the man shouted. 'Speak louder.'

'Shaukas!' Debu yelled as loud as he could. 'Are there any Shaukas here?'

Before the man could reply, a voice rumbled out from the pit. 'Who wants to know about Shaukas?'

Debu stared at the sturdy, weather-beaten figure below him. A beard covered the man's face—much denser than those of the Tibetans, so he could not make out his features too well. But . . . his voice had a familiar ring.

'It's me, Uncle,' Debu began slowly. Then as the man screwed up his eyes to get a better look at him, Debu's heart suddenly came to a standstill. A sharp current tingled through his frame. Was it possible?

'B—Baujyu?' his voice came out in a tearful croak.

'Debu?' His father gasped. 'Debu! Debu! Is it really you?' He shouted so loud that all down the trench miners stopped working to listen. 'What are *you* doing here?'

'Baujyu! It *is* you!' Debu leapt into the furrow. But his father was already rushing up.

'Debu, Debu!' His father squeezed his shoulders, then looked at his face bewildered. 'I can't believe my eyes! Is this real or is it a dream?'

'It's very much real!' Debu laughed, hastily sniffing back his tears, rubbing his face on his father's smelly sheepskin coat. 'Or is it?' He slapped his cheek to make sure. 'It definitely is real. Oh! I just can't believe I've actually found you!' He hugged him again.

'But how did you get here? What are you . . .'

'Doing here? It's a long story, Baujyu. Can we go somewhere quiet and warm? I'm freezing!'

123

'Come along to my tent,' his father said, tugging at his hand. 'We have much to talk about.'

'Friends,' he called out to his fellow workers, who were watching them, their faces wreathed with smiles. 'I'm taking a break.'

The miners held up their shovels and cheered. 'Here, what about your day's pickings?' one yelled. 'Are you celebrating by leaving them for us?'

'Keep them, friends!' Baujyu roared back. 'I have found something worth more than all the gold in the world!'

Debu's throat clamped shut when he heard that. When they had heaved themselves out, Baujyu paused and drew a deep, shuddering breath. 'I still can't believe it,' he whispered. His voice seemed to catch as he asked, 'How are your mother and Hayat?'

'They are all right, Baujyu,' Debu said. 'But have been missing you a great deal.'

His father rubbed his sleeve against his eyes, then folded his hands, looking up to heaven. 'Praise be to our blessed Devi Ma!' He sniffed and went on, 'So have I been missing you all and waiting for the day when we would be reunited.' He looked at Debu again as if to make sure that he actually was there.

Then his mood changed suddenly as he ruffled Debu's hair the way he used to, making his cap fall off, and said in a brighter voice, 'But all that's behind us now, Lord Shiva be praised! Come, we need a strong cup of tea.'

'Your story first!' Baujyu insisted as they sipped the refreshing brew. Dharma Singh exclaimed again and again as he heard about all the mishaps that had befallen Debu. 'Ah,' he finally said. 'Perhaps fate had this in store for you, for all of us. But you took a big risk, son,' he went on. 'This is a difficult country to

125

survive in. But I'm proud of you—really proud.' He was silent for a while. 'I realized that everyone would believe I was dead. And kept wondering how you all were faring.'

Softly, Debu said, 'Yes, everyone had given you up for lost. But . . . I could never accept it . . . Neither could Ma, nor Hayat. And when Sonam Darka appeared with the amulet, I took it for a sign—that I must try to find you.' He paused to flash a happy smile. 'I'm so thankful we didn't give up.'

His father squeezed his arm. 'I don't blame them,' he said. 'It was a terrible storm.'

'But—how did you survive . . . and get here?'

Dharma Singh's face turned grim. 'Well,' he finally replied, 'at first I didn't notice that I'd got separated from the others. I could hear their voices, the sounds the animals were making. But as the storm grew more severe, everything was blotted out. The wind was so fierce, the snow so blinding, it was all I could do to stay on my feet.' He seemed to shrivel at the painful memory. 'I must have taken a wrong turn in the whiteout. And then I realized that I was alone. There was nothing I could do except struggle on. I knew if I stood still or fell down I would freeze to death in no time. Suddenly, I found myself going downhill—but I didn't know that I had turned around in the wrong direction. And then, miraculously, I saw a cave! Somehow, I managed to stagger inside!'

'The caves near Chirchin!' Debu exclaimed.

'The very same. I collapsed as I entered. Fortunately

there was a lama there, meditating. He saved my life. Alone, I'd never have survived.'

'He was the one who took you to his monastery?' Debu asked.

'That was later. He nursed me for several days in the cave itself. The weather was so bad and I was too weak to move.' He caught his breath, then continued. 'When I was better I realized that it was impossible to return home. I was alone, in no condition to make the journey without any animals. Worst, snow had blocked the passes.' He took a deep draught from his cup of tea. 'The lama suggested I go with him to his monastery.'

'But the amulet?' Debu asked. 'When did you sell that?'

'When the weather improved, I took leave of the lama and went to Gartok. However, I had nothing except the few coins on my person. So I decided to go and find Dawa Nangal and ask him to advance me some money or let me take goods on credit. I thought I could make up my losses by trading while I was stranded here in Tibet.'

'What happened then?' Debu asked.

'I discovered that Dawa had passed away and his affairs were in a state of confusion.' Dharma Singh shook his head. 'So I had no choice but to sell my precious amulet, even borrow money to survive. Then I decided to come and work here in the goldfields.'

'So that's what happened,' Debu breathed.

'Anyway,' his father continued, 'now I've made my profit in gold and was planning to return home . . .'

127

'Oh, I wish I'd found you earlier, Baujyu,' Debu exclaimed. 'We could have joined the caravan that left the other day. Uncle Kalyan Singh and the others must be ready to return to Milam. But Tsering said there's another group leaving for Gartok soon.'

'I'll arrange for horses and supplies,' his father replied. 'But first I must meet Tsering and Dolma and thank them for taking such good care of you.'

'Thanks be to Lord Buddha!' Dolma breathed when Debu entered their tent with his father.

'I prayed for you all the time,' Tsering added, smiling shyly.

Dolma cooked a special dinner for them that night. They discovered that Tsering had seen his father at the mine several times but had not realized he was a Shauka. 'I think you were meant to find him yourself,' he said, beaming.

In a few days all the arrangements were made and Debu and his father were ready to leave.

'How can I ever repay your kindness?' Debu said, as Dolma embraced him tearfully and put a small silver charm around his neck for good luck.

'It was our pleasure to have you here with us, however briefly,' Tsering said gruffly, shaking hands with them.

'We will never forget you,' Dharma replied, with a low bow.

As the caravan set off, Debu turned around to take a last look at the goldfields. The wind carried the sound

of the miners' singing and an odd nostalgia tugged at him.

'This place was lucky for us,' his father said. Debu turned to smile at him.

And then it hit him. He had accomplished his dream, found his father! It was all he could do to stop himself from yelling out over and over again, 'I've done it! I've done it!'

OFF TO GARTOK

'I can't wait to see the others' faces,' Debu laughed as his horse trotted alongside his father's. 'They were convinced you were lost in the storm. It was very hard to persuade them to take me along.' Then his face clouded. 'Everything has turned out well, except that I lost Bijli.'

'We'll visit the monastery on our way back,' his father said. 'She'll probably still be there.'

'I just hope so,' Debu said fervently.

They rode fast and reached a large inn by nightfall. As Debu was helping to stable the horses, a warm hand fell on his shoulder.

'Debu? What are you doing here?' It was Sonam Darka!

'Uncle Sonam!' Debu clutched his arm. 'I have wonderful news. I've found my father!'

'You have! Ah, this is the best thing I've heard for a long time.' He hugged Debu. 'It's all due to Lord Buddha's blessings. And your courage and perseverance.'

Just then Debu's father walked out of the inn calling out, 'Debu, Debu!'

'Baujyu, this is Uncle Sonam,' Debu cried, 'the man with the amulet. He has been like another father to me on the trip.'

'Heartiest congratulations to both of you,' Sonam Darka said, shaking Dharma Singh's hand hard. 'You are a lucky man indeed, to have a son like Debu. So brave, so determined and so devoted to you.'

Debu's father bowed his head. 'Many thanks to you, my friend,' he said. 'You were the one who kindled hope in his heart. Debu told me how you helped and encouraged him. But you're right. Debu is an extraordinary boy. Only, I've just discovered it, hmm, Debu?' He smiled and slapped Debu's back playfully.

Debu's face burned with all this unaccustomed praise. Especially from his father, who was not one to hand it out easily. 'But what are you doing here, Uncle?' he blurted out. 'Are the others here too?'

'No . . .' Sonam Darka replied. 'At Gartok I learned that Dharma Singh had gone to the goldfields. So I decided to go there and search, since I'd promised you. But you found him before I did!'

'Let's have dinner together,' Debu's father said, 'and celebrate this reunion.'

They entered the inn and ordered the best meal the place could provide. As they munched steaming-hot meat dumplings, Sonam asked, 'But where exactly did you two find each other? I was so excited to see you that I forgot to ask.'

'The Thok Jalong goldfields, of course,' Debu said, perplexed.

'The goldfields! How did you find out that he was there?' It was Sonam's chance to be puzzled.

'I didn't,' Debu said. He relived his adventures for Sonam Darka, whose face grew more and more serious.

'You must have performed good deeds in your previous birth to survive all that,' he said, shaking his head. 'I have heard of that robber Nangbo. He's quite notorious.'

'Well, the bad times are behind us now,' Dharma Singh said. 'And what about brother Kalyan Singh and the others? Are they still in Gartok?'

'I hope so!' Debu cried. 'We want to go back with them.'

'There's no need to worry,' Sonam said. 'They'll be there for a couple of weeks at least. Kalyan Singh was in two minds whether he should come with me. But I told him that I would send word as soon as I learned anything. What a shock they'll get when they see both of you,' he laughed. 'They think Debu is still at the monastery with the Lama.'

'Well, if I hadn't been captured by the robbers I wouldn't have found you, Baujyu,' Debu said, smiling. 'So it was all for the best, perhaps.'

'Not at all!' Sonam disagreed. 'I would have found him in any case. But—' he stopped abruptly, wrinkling his brow, 'it gave you a chance to test your mettle,' he said.

Dharma Singh nodded. 'You're absolutely right.'

'Will you come back to Gartok with us, Uncle?' Debu asked.

'Of course, I will,' Sonam replied. 'I have no other work at the goldfields. We can watch the horse race together.'

'The Gartok horse race!' Debu cried. 'We'll get a chance to see that?' He'd heard about the famous race. Traditionally the Shauka traders donated fodder and sugar for the horses taking part in it.

After the meal, as Debu suppressed a yawn, Sonam said, 'There's one thing I'm forgetting. Your amulet. Here, take it back, friend.' He began to unwind it from his neck.

'No!' Dharma Singh laid a hand on his arm. 'Keep it. It's lucky, it led Debu to me.'

'Keep it, Uncle,' Debu urged as Sonam hesitated. 'We want you to!'

A REUNION

The journey onwards was much, much pleasanter. The road, though it was full of stones that tried the animals' feet sorely, sloped down to verdant meadows on either side of a stream.

'What are these?' Debu asked, pointing to a large herd of animals, some of which stopped grazing to watch the caravan pass by. They were a bit like horses, only smaller.

'They're kiangs, wild asses,' Sonam said. 'Not much use for riding, their soles are too thin. Some people eat their flesh.'

Packs of hares scampered away from their path. Sometimes they had to cross streams which had no bridges but had to be forded. It was a tricky operation, since they were full of stones and the animals could easily get hurt.

When they finally reached Gartok, Debu discovered it was a small town, with houses built of sun-dried bricks. Prayer poles rose up beside them. And piles of yak dung kept for fuel were heaped here and there.

'The racecourse is outside the town. We'll show it to you tomorrow,' Sonam Darka said. 'All the officials must have come to attend the contest. It's just a couple of days away.'

'And you'll get fresh fish to eat,' Dharma Singh said. 'The river here is full of it.'

'That's something to look forward to!' Debu brightened.

When they reached the camp, Trilok was the first person they saw. The moment he set eyes on Dharma Singh, he went pale, then muttered something and scurried off. Kalyan Singh came hurrying out of his tent in response to Sonam's shout.

He stood stock-still when he saw them, then seemed to be praying under his breath.

'What's the matter?' Dharma Singh cried, folding his hands in greeting. 'You don't look pleased to see me back, brother.'

Kalyan Singh took a deep breath. 'So, it really is you.' He came forward to embrace Dharma Singh. 'Lord Shiva be praised, did you actually survive the storm, or did this boy bring you back to life with his will power?' His wrinkled face was wreathed with smiles. 'It's truly a miracle.'

'A little of both perhaps,' Debu's father said.

'But—' Kalyan Singh began when a loud yell interrupted him. It was Jeevan.

'Ho, Ma! Dharma, brother, is it really you?' Jeevan tossed his cap into the air and caught it again. The other members of their group came running to exclaim and embrace Dharma. And questions flew at him fast and quick!

'Stop, stop!' he laughed. 'I'll tell you the whole story.'

'Trilok here said he'd seen a ghost,' Jeevan laughed. 'I told him he ought to lay off the chhang.'

Trilok came forward reluctantly. Unlike the others' enthusiastic greetings, he shook Dharma Singh's hand jerkily in the Tibetan style.

Then Kalyan Singh said, 'But what is Debu doing here? We had left him behind at the monastery!'

'That's another story which has to be told,' Sonam Darka grinned.

Later, as they sat around the fire, after finishing their frugal dinner of barley flour and dried meat, livened with the fish the men had caught, Debu's father told them how he had survived the blizzard.

'Who could believe it!' Jeevan exclaimed. 'That storm! It was a killer. But, Debu, how did you land up at the goldfields?'

It was Debu's turn to acquaint them with the chain of events that led to their reunion.

'Well,' Kalyan Singh shook his head, 'our people have had all kinds of adventures here. I lost all my goods to robbers once and we have even had to fight off wolves at times. But both your stories are beyond belief.'

'So, Trilok?' Jeevan thumped his back. 'Isn't the boy courageous?' He winked at Debu.

Trilok shrugged. 'L'cky, I th'nk.'

'Just luck can't carry you all the way,' Kalyan Singh's voice was full of reproof. 'Remember how Debu saved your life?'

'You're an ungrateful fellow,' Jeevan muttered as Trilok snorted and walked away. 'But he'll think twice before troubling you now,' he laughed.

Debu smiled. 'Yes, now that Baujyu's back,' he said, 'he won't dare.' He had told his father about Trilok harassing them and Baujyu had said he'd deal with the man at an appropriate time.

'That's not what I meant,' Jeevan replied, his face unusually serious.

Debu wanted to ask what he meant but feared he might sound foolish. Later, however, the remark explained itself. Debu realized that something had changed. He wasn't sure exactly what. Perhaps the way everyone looked at him and spoke to him; not like the child whom they'd indulged and looked after on the journey coming up, but almost like someone who was one of them! It felt strange, and would take some getting used to. He wasn't even sure that he really liked it.

He began to get an inkling when Kalyan Singh said, 'I did not want to bring your son along, Dharma Singh. These journeys are not meant for boys. But I'm glad I don't have to apologize to you for bringing him into danger.'

'So that means I can come every year now?' Debu cried excitedly.

'Maybe,' Dharma Singh said, smiling.

Kalyan Singh stood up and stretched. 'I have to settle your account too, Debu,' he said. 'We'll do that tomorrow.'

As his father frowned questioningly, Debu felt a twinge of unease. 'I—I brought a few things to trade, Baujyu,' he said hurriedly. 'Uncle Kalyan said he'd dispose of them for me when the Lama forced me to stay back at the monastery.'

'Things to trade? That was a clever thing to do,' his father said slowly. 'How did you manage it?'

'Well—I did it somehow . . .' Debu's voice trailed away. Suddenly the feeling of being grown-up and important vanished. His stomach felt hollow as apprehension gripped him. He pretended to yawn loudly.

'It's late,' his father said. 'You can tell me tomorrow.'

But that felt like small comfort as Debu plodded to the tent they were to occupy. What would Baujyu say if he told him that they had dug up the tankas he had concealed in the ground, even a couple of gold coins? Would he be angry? Had he displayed too much initiative?

A CONFESSION

'We might have left for Milam by now,' Kalyan Singh said, the next morning, to Dharma Singh. 'But when Sonam told us that he'd heard you were still alive and had gone to Thok Jalong we thought we should wait.' He smiled wryly. 'Frankly, I didn't have much hope. But he insisted, and I too felt we must, for the boy's sake.'

Jeevan nodded. 'Yes, all of us felt it was important . . . The weather hasn't been too bad this year,' he continued. 'And then, we thought we could watch the horse race too.'

'It will be held tomorrow,' Sonam smiled. 'But we can show you the racecourse today.' He threw a keen look at Debu. 'What's the matter? Are you feeling all right?'

'I—I'm perfectly fine, Uncle,' Debu stammered.

'He's been quiet since the morning,' Jeevan said. 'You can rest in the tent if you want to.'

'No—no,' Debu said.

Kalyan Singh stood up and cleared his throat. 'Come, let me give you your account,' he said. Baujyu nodded. Reluctantly Debu rose and followed them, his mouth dry as a day-old chapatti. What if his father scolded him in front of all the others? All that hard-earned respect and admiration would vanish. How unbearable it would be! But what could he do? Frantically, he cast about in his mind . . . He had to take Baujyu aside and tell him, instead of letting him discover it by chance.

He tugged at his father's sleeve, and gestured to him to turn aside. 'What is it?' Dharma Singh asked. Debu's heart plunged. He hadn't noticed before how fierce and menacing the beard that covered his father's face now, made him look.

He swallowed, drew his tongue over his frozen lips. 'Baujyu,' he said, 'I want to tell you something.'

His father stared at him. 'What is it?' he asked.

'When they allowed me to come along on the expedition, I felt I should carry some goods, so that the expense of the trip could be recovered. But—we were barely managing as it is. So—' he said, not daring to look at Baujyu's face. 'I—I dug up that pot you had buried in the ground . . . and took out some coins to buy goods . . . also to sell them here. I know I shouldn't have done it,' he pleaded, 'but there seemed no other way. Things were pretty hard . . . without you.' To his horror he felt tears gathering in his eyes.

141

He heard his father's breath catch. 'How . . . did you know they were there?'

'I—I saw you hiding something one night . . .' Debu went on in a rush. 'When I decided to take goods to trade I thought I should contact your partner Dawa Nangal. But I was afraid he might not acknowledge me. I began to search for the stone that was the proof of your partnership . . . Instead I found the pot of coins. '

Kalyan Singh's shout burst through the silence. 'Aren't you coming, you two? You can always catch up on other things later. Let me get rid of this responsibility.'

Debu glanced up. But his father's face was expressionless. Finally Baujyu sighed and touched him lightly on his shoulder. 'Come,' he said. 'Let us see what account Kalyan Singh has to give us.'

Debu stumbled behind him, relieved.

Luckily Kalyan Singh had managed to get a good rate for the tankas. He had traded some of the other goods for salt and wool. 'I knew your mother would be happy to get wool, the rate is so much lower here. And the salt you can sell for a good profit back home. Anyway . . .' he glanced up at Dharma Singh, 'now your father's here, he can decide what's best.'

He looked at Dharma Singh again, uncertainly. 'I hope you are satisfied, Dharma, with this trade.'

'How can I not be satisfied?' Debu felt an enormous load lift when his father's face creased into a smile at last. 'All the losses I suffered last year are almost recovered—thanks to you and—this—this inquisitive boy.' Debu could have collapsed, he was so delighted.

'And now it's time to visit the racecourse,' Sonam · Darka said behind them.

'You take the boy,' Dharma Singh said. 'I want to go and buy some goods with this money. And there's another problem . . . Since Dawa Nangal has passed away, I am without a partner. I have to do something about that too.'

Debu left silently with Sonam Darka. For some reason the prospect of going to the racecourse did not seem so exciting any more. He would have liked to go with his father to the marketplace and see what it was like.

'We can come back and see the markets after we've been to the racecourse,' Sonam Darka said, as they saddled their horses.

'Uncle Sonam, you seem to know everything without my telling you,' Debu cried.

'Because I have a boy too, as I told you,' Sonam said. 'If there had been time I would have taken you to my village to meet him . . . Maybe some other time.'

'Promise, Uncle?' Debu cried, as the pony began to trot along on the road that led out of the city.

A BOLT OF LIGHTNING!

'The racecourse is about four miles long,' Sonam said, as they stood looking at a wide expanse of plain. 'They take care to maintain it well and see that there are no stones to obstruct the horses. There's a stream too that the contestants have to cross.'

An untidy bunch of horses was sweeping towards them. It was the contenders practising for the race.

'The riders look very young,' Debu remarked.

'Usually boys around twelve are chosen,' Sonam said. 'They are lighter in weight and so the horses can run faster. And they all come from Rudok, like the horses.'

'Like my Bijli!' Debu exclaimed. His eyes widened, 'Oh, there's a horse which looks just like her.'

As he spoke, the horses came thundering up to them. Debu leaned over to get a better look. 'Hai Rama!'

he cried out. 'If I didn't know better, I could have sworn it was Bijli herself!'

The words were barely out of his mouth when he heard a familiar neigh. The pony jerked its head violently and reared up on its hind legs. To his horror, the rider was thrown off! Luckily he fell on the outer side of the track, away from the galloping hooves behind him. Debu and Sonam jumped off and ran to pick him up.

As Debu bent to help the boy, he felt something warm nuzzling his neck. His breath caught. 'It—it really is Bijli!' he cried, stroking her neck, as she whinnied again and again. Just then the boy groaned loudly. Some of the men standing nearby came rushing up. One of them turned and said something in an angry voice. Sonam replied as sharply.

'What's the matter?' Debu asked.

'He says we made the horse bolt and throw its rider!' Sonam replied.

'But that's not true!' Debu cried. 'We were standing here quietly.'

Fortunately, by that time some of the other riders returned to confirm their statement. And thankfully the boy had not broken any bones, as they'd feared, though he'd twisted his ankle when he fell.

'But what is Bijli doing here?' Debu asked. 'I'll try and find out later,' Sonam Darka said. 'It's better that we leave right now. Come,' he pulled Debu away and quickly mounted his horse.

Unwillingly Debu followed suit. Bijli's whinnies of protest as one of the men led her away echoed painfully in his ears.

Sonam Darka rode so fast that there was no chance of asking him for an explanation. Debu had a hard time keeping up. When they had put a safe distance between themselves and the racecourse, Sonam slowed down to a comfortable trot.

'I'm sorry I dragged you away like that, but we could have gotten into serious trouble,' he said, his face grim.

'But why? The others also agreed we did nothing,' Debu protested.

'I'm afraid the matter has become complicated. The man who accused us claims that we bewitched the horse, because she came up to you!'

'But it was Bijli! I am absolutely sure. She came up to me because she recognized me.'

'They will never agree to that. You see, she belongs to the Garphan now.'

'The Garphan!' Debu cried out in dismay. The Garphan was a very important official, the representative of the Lhasa government, in charge of the whole area. 'How did he come to own her? Surely the Lama couldn't have sold her or given her away?'

'Who knows what happened?' Sonam said with a sigh. 'If your father has finished his business, it might be better for you to leave right away.'

'And miss the race?' Debu exclaimed, disappointed. And leave Bijli behind? he thought to himself.

'You'll be lucky if you escape without severe punishment,' Sonam said. 'Though I don't think she's one of his top ponies. He wouldn't enter an untried one. But they must consider her good enough to attempt one of the secondary prizes.'

146

The others had returned from the market and Debu's father looked quite cheerful. He greeted them loudly. 'You did a clever thing, Debu,' he said, 'bringing those tankas. We got an excellent rate this year.'

Debu tried to smile and nod. Canny Kalyan Singh sensed the tension in the air. He threw a questioning glance at Sonam who drew him aside.

'So,' Dharma Singh asked. 'What did you think of the racecourse?'

'It was very impressive,' Debu said, trying to ignore the sound of Sonam's voice as he and Kalyan conferred in low tones.

Then he noticed his father examining him intently. 'There's something wrong,' he said, and his gaze travelled to Sonam Darka and Kalyan Singh, taking note of their anxious expressions. 'What happened?'

It all came out in a rush. How he had seen Bijli and she had recognized him and thrown her rider, and how some of the onlookers had blamed them for it.

Just then Kalyan Singh drew closer and asked, 'Have you heard, Dharma Singh?'

Debu's father nodded. 'It would probably be best to pack up and leave right away,' Kalyan Singh said. 'Even if they don't do anything now, if Bijli doesn't win anything in the races, they might turn around and blame us for bewitching her.'

'You are right,' Bijay Singh added. 'This Garphan is quite whimsical. Even the local landowners are careful not to offend him. He might feel insulted if his horse doesn't get a prize. He could punish Debu for practising black magic and might even confiscate our goods. We should slip away quietly.'

'Why sh'ld we slip away quietly?' It was Trilok Singh. 'Why sh'ld we miss the races bec'se of this boy's foolishness? It's entirely your fault for br'ng'ng him, Kalyan Singh. We've had no end of trouble bec'se of him, and st'll you'll keep praising him, givin' him a swollen head. If I'd been his father I'd give him a good hamm'ring, teach him to resp'ct his elders.'

Debu heart lurched as a red light jumped into his father's eyes. 'You . . . good-for-nothing, how dare you!' He lunged at Trilok.

'Baujyu!' Debu threw himself at him. 'Ignore him. He's not worth it. We can't waste time fighting.'

'The boy is right,' Kalyan Singh said. 'We don't have time to waste. And you, Trilok, if you don't want to come with us, no one's stopping you from staying on. Let's get ready to leave,' he told the others.

'So you're pr'pared to sacr'f'ce us because of the boy,' Trilok snarled. 'I'll rem'mber this, Kalyan Singh. Let's see what the headman has to say about it.'

'There are many things the headman will have to know about,' Kalyan Singh replied contemptuously. 'I'll be too happy to tell him.'

'I think all of us will,' Jeevan added. His jovial face turned hard. 'I'm not staying here to face the Garphan's wrath. We're not sacrificing anything more than a race.'

Bijay Singh nodded vigorously. 'It would be stupid to risk all our gains,' he said, turning away.

Trilok Singh glared at them, then threw down his hookah. The rest of them rushed into their tents and began to fling their belongings together hurriedly, then load the pack animals as fast as they could.

They were almost ready to leave when they heard a loud voice call out, 'Where is Kalyan Singh? Where's the leader of this group?'

'Stay here, Debu,' Kalyan Singh whispered. 'I'll see what it is.'

He strode out asking, 'Who's looking for me?' But Debu couldn't resist peeping through an opening in the tent. He had to know what was going on.

A man in long robes stood there. 'The Garphan wants to see you,' he said.

'What business does the Garphan have with me?' Kalyan Singh asked. 'Hasn't the fodder and sugar we sent for the racehorses reached? Or is it less than the quantity that is required? Please let me know so that I can send some more.'

'No,' said the man. 'It is nothing like that.'

'What is it then?' Kalyan Singh said smoothly. 'Can we humble traders be of help to the mighty Garphan in any way? I would have come right away—not wasted time in questions, but one of our party is ill. And I'm the only one who has enough knowledge of herbs to help him, so I have to attend to him.'

The man frowned suspiciously. He was about to speak when Kalyan Singh took something out from his pocket. He opened his palm and said, looking at it, 'This is a piece of turquoise I have saved. It is of excellent quality. Would His Excellency appreciate something like this?'

The man's hand swooped on the large turquoise

149

bead and grabbed it. 'What use would the great Garphan have for a little lump of turquoise? He has hundreds like these.' He beckoned to Kalyan to come close and muttered something in his ear.

'Is that all?' Kalyan looked relieved. 'Hmmm, I think I'll ask someone else to administer the dose to the sick man. Tell the Garphan I'm coming, along with the boy.'

A shiver ran down Debu's back. Why had Kalyan Singh agreed to take him to the Garphan? He had to run away, hide! He was about to slip through the opening on the other side of the tent when someone entered. It was his father.

'Kalyan Singh says the Garphan has sent for you,' he said slowly. 'I'm not sure if you should go. But he feels there's nothing to worry about.'

'I don't want to go!' Debu cried. 'Suppose he punishes me?'

'If he wanted to punish you, he wouldn't have summoned you in this way.' It was Sonam Darka. 'He would have had you picked up by his men, not sent for you. I would advise you to go and pay your respects.'

Kalyan Singh had entered too. 'He is right,' he said. 'Come, Debu. Let us not waste any more time.'

Despite all this reassurance, Debu was quaking inwardly as they approached the Garphan's house.

It was much larger than the others he had seen, a long building with a three-tiered roof covered with fluttering prayer flags, which made it a riot of colour and movement.

Strips of bright silk were strung over the main door, and the red doorposts were overlaid with intricate

150

designs. A servant ushered them in and Debu tried to ignore the goosebumps crawling like ants on his skin. He glanced around surreptitiously, taking in the patterns of flowers, trees, animals—even an elephant—which ornamented the walls. There was also one that looked like a scene of the horse race!

A tall thin man, with a humorous looking face, was sitting on a carved chair with another attendant standing behind him. A low table painted with dragons was placed before him. A wispy moustache drooped on either side of his thin lips and a large turquoise earring dangled from one ear. He was dressed in the Chinese style, like all the important officials, and wore a yellow hat with a handle and a yellow tassel attached to it with a large blue button. Later Kalyan Singh told him that it indicated his rank. And also that it was the third in the state.

Kalyan Singh removed his cap; Debu followed suit. He bowed low and shook hands with the Garphan. They were asked to sit down. 'So how has trade been?' the Garphan asked.

'Good as usual, thanks to your kind favour,' Kalyan Singh answered. 'I hope the fodder and sugar we sent for the horses is of a quality good enough to satisfy Your Excellency.'

The Garphan nodded. 'It is satisfactory,' he said.

A servant came in and offered them tea in cups made of green stone, smoothly polished. Kalyan took one sip and put it back. Debu, who had picked up the cup gingerly—it looked quite valuable—did the same. He sensed that a certain etiquette was to be observed.

151

But the Garphan's eyes had been fixed on him throughout and he was growing more and more uncomfortable.

'How old is the boy?' he asked.

'I believe he has completed fourteen years,' Kalyan Singh replied.

'Hmmm . . .' The Garphan examined Debu some more, then said, 'He's little too old . . . but I have been told he is good with horses.'

Kalyan Singh spread his hands. 'Our children practically grow up on horses,' he said. He paused and threw a shrewd glance at the Garphan. 'If he could be of any use to Your Excellency . . . he would be most willing.'

The Garphan sighed then grunted again. 'Perhaps he could . . .' he stroked his chin thoughtfully. Debu noticed that the nails of his little fingers were extraordinarily long. Then he said, 'One of my horses is without a rider.' His eyes narrowed. 'He fell off his horse and hurt himself while he was practising yesterday . . . I have heard you were there, boy?'

Kalyan threw a warning glance at Debu and said quickly, 'I heard about that incident, Your Excellency. They were simply watching them practice when it happened.'

'Is that so?' The Garphan fingered his moustache. 'They say the horse threw off the rider and ran to you as if bewitched. Hunhh?'

'Your Excellency—' Debu started up.

But before he could continue, Kalyan Singh butted in saying, 'He has a way with horses, he was born with it. Sometimes it creates problems. Once a horse followed him and the owner thought we had stolen it.'

'Is that so?' The Garphan repeated again. Then burst into high-pitched laughter. 'A way with horses—he-he-he!' The attendant began to laugh too and so did Kalyan and Debu—though he had to force his laughter out.

The Garphan's mirth died away finally and he beckoned for more tea, which they sipped and put back again. Why doesn't he say what he wants? Debu thought. The suspense was unbearable. But he had a faint inkling of what it could be.

And sure enough, the Garphan finally said, 'If he's so proficient with horses, then he should be able to ride that pony for me in the race . . .'

Ride Bijli? Debu almost jumped up to say 'Yes!'.

But again Kalyan Singh spoke before he could and his words puzzled him. 'He would be deeply honoured, Your Excellency. But the pony seems to throw its riders, they say. Not that he is afraid to risk injury,' he went on, 'if Your Excellency requires his services. But suppose the horse does not cooperate and loses the race?'

The Garphan smiled thinly. 'Hmmm . . . It is a new horse, but an excellent one, I was told, that was why I was advised to buy it. I am just trying it out. I do not expect it to win the top prize the first time. But I do wish to find out what it is capable of.' He turned to Debu and said, 'Do you think you can ride it, boy?'

Debu took a deep breath. 'I would be deeply honoured, Your Excellency,' he said, bowing.

THE RACE

It was a very different Debu who returned to the camp. Pride, excitement, longing battled inside him, along with a growing anxiety. To ride in the horse race! He'd never done anything like it before. True, he and his friends had raced horses for fun. But that was a game, child's play. And then, Bijli had never raced competitively, for a major award.

'I didn't want you to agree right away,' Kalyan Singh broke into his thoughts. 'We had to make it clear that we could not guarantee that you would win the race. It's a matter of great prestige for the officials that their horses win.'

'I didn't realize that,' Debu said ruefully.

'Never mind,' Kalyan Singh said. 'We made him admit that he was not expecting an extraordinary performance from you and Bijli. I think he was so keen to find a suitable rider that he decided to overlook the accusation that you bewitched her. In fact, I suspect he chose you for that very reason.'

'You really think so?' Debu laughed. Then his mouth drooped again. 'He thinks I'll charm Bijli and win the race? But . . . I'll never get Bijli back now,' he said despondently.

'Let's see how things go tomorrow,' Kalyan Singh said. 'For all you know, he may not be too keen to keep a bewitched pony.'

'I just hope so,' Debu said. 'But what is the prize, Uncle?'

'The first prize is a pony of the best quality, the second a good yak and so on. And the person who comes last gets a prize too!' Kalyan Singh smiled.

'That is really kind of them. What is it?' Debu asked.

'A basket of dung!' Kalyan Singh's laugh sounded like a rusty hinge, as if he were out of practice. Debu joined in heartily.

'That's not so bad, Uncle,' he said when he caught his breath again. 'A basket of dung can be put to good use.'

'Definitely,' Kalyan Singh wiped his streaming eyes. 'After all, it is useful as fuel.'

Dharma Singh and the others were waiting for them anxiously. But one look at Kalyan Singh and Debu's faces reassured them.

'I told you,' Sonam said. 'If he had been angry with you he would have behaved differently.'

'But I'm not sure if I like the idea—Debu taking part in the race,' Dharma Singh said.

155

'You don't have much choice,' Jeevan pointed out.

Dharma Singh nodded reluctantly. But as for Debu, there was only one thought in his mind: how could he get Bijli back?

Sonam Darka accompanied Debu the next morning, as a pale, sharp light fanned out into the sky from behind the distant hills. They rode silently. Debu watched the smoke spiralling up from behind the little houses, the prayer flags fluttering in the wind.

He almost didn't recognize Bijli. She was decked out with green and pink ribbons. Red tassels and tinkling bells hung from her neck. The end of her tail had been braided neatly and a bright new rug covered her back. She whinnied loudly in greeting and tossed her head so hard that the man who was holding her stepped back, startled. Many of the ponies had been similarly decorated for the race. As Debu drew closer to stroke her neck, the other riders stared at him and whispered to each other. Some of the boys looked frightened, the others sullen.

'Don't worry about anything,' Sonam Darka said. 'Just do your best.' Debu nodded and tried to smile despite the nervousness that suddenly gripped him. How would the result of the race affect them? And— would this be the last time he rode Bijli?

Trying to calm himself, Debu swung himself onto Bijli's back. A cold wind stung his cheeks, though the sun was bright. The other boys were already lining up and he followed suit. Absent-mindedly, he watched the heads ahead of him, some short-cropped, others with hanging pigtails, still others with plaits wrapped around their heads. The deep maroon, yellow and red coats the riders wore stood out starkly against the dazzling blue sky. The fresh smell of grass, trampled under the horses' restless feet tickled his nostrils, mingled with the rich odour of earth.

Dimly Debu heard the buzz of the spectators' voices over the jingling of the horses' bells, glimpsed the wall of tents beyond the racecourse and the violet mountains behind them. He could not bring himself to glance at the watching crowd, though he knew that his father and his companions must be there. He could only respond with a jerky nod to Sonam's final words of encouragement, shouted behind him as he rode forward.

He shifted uncomfortably. The saddle was different from the type he was used to. Another obstacle, though he had been told that the lightest saddles were used to help the horses achieve maximum speed.

It was a four-mile course, Debu remembered. Would Bijli be able to run that far? The playful races back home were hardly any training for this. And while the difficult journey might have built up her stamina, Bijli could be stubborn and self-willed. He remembered how she had slowed down petulantly once, just when he was winning, because he spoke harshly to her. After that he took care to control his temper, and coax her with loving words.

The other riders had an advantage—they were much lighter. How humiliating it would be to lose to children . . . A creditable showing might satisfy the Garphan, but he couldn't believe what Kalyan Singh had suggested. That he might let Debu take Bijli back because he may not want to keep a bewitched horse. There was one possibility . . . however . . . if they won the race . . . which seemed almost impossible right now . . .

The tension had gotten to Bijli too. She was trembling, jerking her head about. It seemed she didn't like this place, didn't want to be here.

A sharp exclamation brought Debu back to reality. Bijli had moved too close to another horse. He looked into the sharp bony face of the rider, a boy with a sloping forehead, mounted on a handsome black steed. Debu forced his stiff lips into a smile but received a dark scowl in response. He took a deep breath and murmured the words he always used to encourage Bijli back home. 'Come on, my lightning bolt, live up to your name.'

To his dismay, Bijli drummed her feet and tugged at the reins defiantly. Desperately Debu tried again,

'You have to do it, my Bijli,' he repeated, in the softest, most loving tone he could muster. 'Just do it once, speed like lightning, leave all the others far behind and I promise you, we'll go home right away. Home to Hayat and Ma . . .'

Was it Hayat's name that did the trick, he wondered. Did it remind her of the home they'd left behind and were eager to return to? That very moment the gunshot that was the signal to start boomed in his ear. And Bijli's response made him gasp. She shot forward, along with the other horses, like the lightning she'd been named after.

'Come on, Debu! Get in front!' Was that Baujyu's voice shouting above the others? The mass of waving sleeves was a blur, as he sped past the spectators.

The black horse ridden by the boy with the bony face was in the lead. Bijli was racing neck to neck with a bunch of ponies in the middle ranks. 'We have to work our way up!' Debu muttered, watching the manes flying in front of him.

Immediately Bijli quickened her pace. The thud of hooves hammered at Debu's ear, the swishing of whips, the shrill exclamations of the boys goading their steeds on. Slowly, steadily, they left one horse behind, then another, then another. And now they had reached fourth place!

'Keep it up, my lightning bolt,' Debu murmured, pressing his foot lightly into her side. 'You're doing very well.'

The black stallion was maintaining the first place, though the others were trying to catch up. He could

160

hear the boy ahead screaming at his horse, whipping it on.

'That's the way,' Debu whispered to Bijli. 'Keep it up and we'll surely win.' Right now it was important only to retain their place. The winning burst of speed would have to come later. But how much ground had they covered? He did not know the racecourse—would just have to guess.

Suddenly the stream they had to cross reared up. He heard a high, excited shriek as the pony who was in second place surged ahead to catch up with the black one. A dangerous place to pick up speed Debu thought, even though it was a small stream. In a way it was a clever tactic because the horses automatically slowed down there. The two were off again, racing neck to neck, when the third contestant whipped his pony, sharply urged it forward. But in its eagerness to get ahead, the horse lost its footing on the slippery pebbles and fell straight in Debu's path!

'Bijli!' Debu shrieked. He rose in the stirrups, braced himself for the fall. But instead he found himself soaring in the air as they vaulted effortlessly over the fallen steed!

'Bijli,' he whispered breathlessly, 'where did you learn to jump like that?'

Bijli did not bother to reply. She was concentrating on winning the race. She was flying like the wind as she streaked past the others, leaving their pounding hooves far behind. And then—was that the winning post? Debu went slack with relief. But the next moment his breath stopped—hooves were hammering

161

unbearably close to them. He heard the hoarse breathing, the harsh cries of a rider striving to catch up, beat them to the goal.

'Come on, Bijli!' he coaxed, as he glimpsed a black head from the corner of his eye. 'Just a little faster!'

Bijli tossed her head proudly, setting all her bells a-jingle. She exploded into a burst of speed with the force of a gale. The hoof beats grew faint behind them.

And—the winning post flashed up before them! The blood roared in Debu's ears as they thundered past. He saw the officials' excited faces, their waving silk sleeves, but could not hear what their open mouths said. Bijli might have run on if he hadn't gathered his wits to tug at the reins and whisper hoarsely, 'Stop, Bijli, stop! We've done it! We've done it!'

Now the congratulatory shouts erupted in a deafening clamour. Someone grabbed the reins, someone else reached out to hold his numb hands, but he was already scrambling off Bijli's back. He paused to embrace her neck for a moment, before he was pulled away.

It all went by in a blur, the cheers, the hugs, the pats on the back. Had he actually won the race? Debu's throat was raw and his eyes burned as they watched Bijli being dragged away, her neighs of protest filling his ears. His companions' praise, even his father's delight could not warm him.

THE PRIZE

'The Garphan is very pleased,' Kalyan Singh said, beaming. 'You have brought much honour to our people!'

The great man stood there before him, his smile stretching almost to his ears. 'I knew you could do it, boy!' he cried. 'I know how to pick a winner.' He shook Debu's hands till Debu felt he might just tear them off.

'Your Excellency has impeccable judgement,' Kalyan Singh said, bowing. He nudged Debu to do the same.

'Hmmph—but you had doubts, my man,' the Garphan waggled a finger. 'But come along. You are all permitted to join us for the display.'

Reluctantly Debu followed him on to the raised platform below the large colourful tent meant for privileged spectators and took a seat. Baujyu sat down beside him saying, 'This will be an experience to remember. They perform wonderful feats of horsemanship. Not that yours was any less!' Debu tried hard to smile.

He heard drumbeats and the mournful blare of trumpets. And then a pony with a brilliant red harness galloped up at full speed. What's so extraordinary, he thought, when suddenly the rider rose up and in one smooth, swift movement stood on his head on the horse's back! The crowd gasped.

'Have you ever seen anything like this?' Baujyu cried, clapping as excitedly as a young boy.

Debu could only nod. Bijli's bewildered whinnies as she was led away still rang in his ears. He heard Jeevan's sharp whistle as another pony thundered past, then reared up and danced merrily in time to the music on its hind legs.

It was followed by another. Dazed, he stared as the horseman galloped past, took aim with one of the two guns slung on his shoulders, and heard the deafening blast as he fired it. The bullet had barely reached its mark when the second gun exploded. The crowd cheered loudly—both shots had found their target. Another horse hurtled on to the scene and two more shots rang out. But this time there was a disappointed murmur. One of them fell short.

'Now they'll display their skill in archery,' Baujyu said. 'They are quite extraordinary. Did I tell you that their generals are titled Lords of the Arrow?'

Debu shook his head. Even as his father spoke, another horseman rode up at incredible speed. Despite his preoccupation, Debu was beginning to get carried away by the excitement throbbing in the air. He watched enthralled as the rider half rose and swiftly fitted an arrow to his bow, which whizzed close to the target with a loud 'thuk' and followed it with a gun shot. Another archer followed and achieved a better shot. However, Debu's thoughts were slipping away again.

He would be receiving a beautiful pony as a prize, he had been told. But would the Garphan agree to the exchange? Suppose he got offended?

'Debu, Debu!' His father jogged his elbow. 'The prize distribution is beginning.' Debu blinked. The dust from the horses' hooves still clouded the air but the crowd had hushed its clamour.

'Haven't you heard, Debu?' Kalyan Singh sounded irritable. 'The Garphan is calling you to receive your prize.'

Debu followed him, as mechanically as a puppet. 'I know why you're upset, son,' Kalyan Singh whispered. 'But I thought you would be able to cope with this too. You're one of the bravest boys I've ever seen.'

I'm tired of being brave, Debu thought. Why does it have to be like this? I found Baujyu, but I have to lose Bijli. Why can't I have both?

A beautiful pony was being led forward, bedecked even more elaborately than Bijli had been. A silver-grey pony, the same colour as Bijli, with a silken mane. Debu heard the cheers and shouts around him as he took the reins from the Garphan with leaden hands and bowed to him.

Then he took a deep breath. It was time to make his last try. His mouth felt as if he had swallowed a huge lump of barley flour without tea to wash it down, and his heart pumped like the blacksmith's bellows, but he had to do it.

He had just opened his mouth, when the Garphan said something, but the words were lost in the cry that went up from the crowd. Not a cry of congratulation, but surprise and alarm. He swung around to see what was happening.

It was Bijli! Bijli was galloping at full speed, evading the stable hands chasing her. Bijli, whinnying, racing round and round in circles as the frightened crowd scattered. Debu heard the Garphan's voice raised in command and the agitated yells of the other officials who were seated on the platform.

'Bijli,' he called. 'Bijli!'

She heard him over the other voices, paused, arrested her wild cavorting and trotted up through the melee to nuzzle his face.

Debu felt the tears course down his cheeks no matter how hard he tried to control them. What would Baujyu and the others say? He was about to bury his face in Bijli's neck when a rough hand pulled him away. It was the Garphan's attendant.

Debu shrugged the man's hand off his shoulder and was about to let his rage burst forth, when a sudden thought jerked it back. He collected himself, then turned to the Garphan who stood there, his face a mask of astonishment and fear, surrounded by gesturing, babbling officials.

When Debu spoke, his voice was calm. 'Your Excellency, please forgive this foolish horse. She is only an animal, and seems to have become unduly attached to me . . .' He knelt and said with folded hands, 'It is very presumptuous to make this request, but I know Your Excellency is magnanimous and merciful. I beg you to allow me to relieve you of this troublesome steed!' Disregarding the amazement that drew the Garphan's fine brows together, the officials' horrified gasps, he sprang to his feet, grabbed the reins of the prize horse and said, 'And offer this beautiful pony in exchange?'

For a long moment the Garphan's gaze bored into him. Debu kept his own eyes downcast. He could hear agitated whispers all around him, punctuated with guttural sounds of disapproval.

Then the Garphan's voice rang out. 'You are right, boy, the horse is unreliable.' His lip curled, 'She has no respect for authority. You are welcome to take her as the prize. I will keep the better horse—as befits my station.'

Debu grasped the Garphan's hand and touched it to his forehead. 'Your Excellency is truly great,' he cried.

Kalyan Singh added, 'What more can I say, Your Excellency, but that we will return home singing your praises? Seldom have I witnessed such generosity.'

When the crowd had settled down again and the other prizes began to be announced, the little group slipped away.

Their belongings had been packed, the goods were being loaded on the pack animals. Debu was chasing a particularly unruly yak when he heard a sharp whistle

and the loud thud of a stone-sling finding its mark.
The startled animal stopped in its tracks and Sonam
Darka leaped forward to grasp its horns.

'Thank you, Uncle,' Debu grinned, quickly piling
his bags of borax on the animal's back, and tying
them securely. 'I should have remembered what you
taught me.'

Sonam Darka laughed and thumped his back. 'You don't need any more lessons. You managed to persuade the great Garphan himself to do what you wanted.'

'That was quite daring,' Bijay Singh said, as he rolled a blanket. 'But I think the Garphan seriously believed you had bewitched Bijli.'

'He's a wise man,' Jeevan laughed, pulling up the tent stakes. 'But our Debu is no less. He knows how to drive a bargain—as befits a trader.'

'I thought it was only fair to offer him the prize pony,' Debu said, 'since he had paid good money for Bijli.'

'So, Debu, your first trip augurs well for the future,' Sonam Darka's sunburnt face crinkled in an enormous smile. 'You succeeded in finding your father and won the race as well.'

'And got my beloved Bijli back,' Debu smiled. 'Thanks to your good wishes and prayers for me, Uncle.' His voice was sombre as he said softly, 'I will miss you.'

'And I will miss you too,' Sonam too turned serious.

'But I have something to tell you, Debu,' his father said. 'Something that'll make you very happy. You know I had to find a new partner . . . Guess who my new mitra, my representative here is . . .?'

Debu jumped up to hug Sonam Darka. 'I know— and cannot imagine anyone better, Baujyu!' he exclaimed.

Sonam Darka nodded too as he squeezed Debu's shoulder.

'We must hurry!' Kalyan Singh bustled up. 'It's not a good time to leave, as it is we'll have to camp on the roadside.'

'I don't think the merciful Buddha will try you further,' Sonam said. 'But yes, you should be on your way.'

What a journey it had been, Debu thought as the caravan began to move out of Gartok. Right now it seemed like a dream. The Lama, Nangbo, Dolma and Tsering, had they all existed? He fingered the silver charm Dolma had insisted on tying around his neck for good luck, to assure himself they had. What a lot he had to tell his mother, Hayat and his friends in the village!

The sun was losing heat, but the glare still bounced off the white ground. Debu pulled the fur-rimmed hat Sonam had insisted he keep, over his eyes. He looked at the road winding ahead, the light brushing the snow-capped mountains with a silvery sheen, and exhilaration gripped him. He remembered how he had set off from Milam—trembling with hope and dread, torn between excitement and fear. And the return—what a contrast it was! It was as if he had lived an age between the two, as if it were someone else going back, not the Debu who'd started out. As he turned to exchange a smile with his father, he visualized his mother's look of overjoyed surprise, heard Hayat's welcoming yell.

Suddenly Kalyan Singh broke into the chant 'Hari Om!' and his father's light baritone took it up. When the others chimed in, Debu felt as if they had flown over the high mountains like the Shaukia Lama and were already home. Gratefully he added his voice to theirs.